I0681227

MURDER IN
JACKSON HOLE

MURDER IN JACKSON HOLE

MAUDE PARKER

COACHWHIP PUBLICATIONS

Greenville, Ohio

Murder in Jackson Hole, by Maude Parker
© 2021 Coachwhip Publications edition

Front cover: Tetons © TWildlife / Cowboy © Ednal

First published 1955
Maude Pavenstedt, 1892-1959, wrote under her maiden
    name, Maude Parker. Born in Galveston, Texas, she
    studied at the University of Wisconsin. She married
    Richard Washburn Child, who became ambassador to
    Italy (and she wrote about her experiences there as
    Mussolini rose to power). She later married New York
    lawyer Edmund W. Pavenstedt. She wrote ten books,
    most being mysteries.
CoachwhipBooks.com

ISBN 1-61646-503-4
ISBN-13 978-1-61646-503-2

1

"This is as close to Paradise as I ever expect to get," I said, settling myself into one of the long porch chairs of rawhide.

No one was within sight. Jim bent down and kissed me.

"The landscape's not bad either," he said presently.

And after a moment I turned my attention to the external Paradise: the glorious blue of the Wyoming summer sky, the distant snow-topped peak of the Grand Teton; and near at hand, within the confines of the small dude ranch itself, picturesque well-kept log cabins, tree-shaded, bright with flowers. Beyond the restful stretch of green lawn, dazzling silver marked the turbulent waters of the Snake, glistening in the noonday sun.

I glanced again at Jim; six foot two, lean of build, deeply sun-tanned, he looked his best in Levi's and a tieless white shirt, sleeves rolled above the elbow. He looked younger than his thirty-three years, too, now that two thirds of the continent separated him from the New York law offices of his nonvacation days.

"I almost wish David Ferensen weren't coming," I said lazily, in the blissful somnolence of supreme well-being. I'd all but fallen asleep just now in a sybaritically warm bath after three hours of vigorous riding earlier this morning.

"Oh, you'll like David."

Jim spoke with assurance. He'd done a great deal of legal work for David Ferensen, momentarily due to arrive by car from Ohio with his daughter and a young business associate who served nominally as secretary.

Usually I like the people Jim likes. Usually I'm favorably inclined toward self-made men. But for reasons I preferred not to analyze I had mental reservations about this outstandingly successful industrialist.

I hedged by saying, "But it's so peaceful as it is now."

Laughter began in Jim's dark-browed hazel eyes, spilled over into sound. "And how long would it stay peaceful, my darling, if David didn't come?"

I glanced toward the kitchen wing of the main cabin where Mary Sloan doubtless was preparing luncheon. "It would be a catastrophe for Mary," I said soberly, awake now, the spell broken.

"And for Brad and Susan, too," I added. Privately, though, I regarded Mary's welfare as even more important than the welfare of her husband or of their daughter, which was saying a good deal. I'd known them only two weeks in calendar time, but two weeks of communal living here was the equivalent of ten years in city terms.

"I suppose some idiosyncratic soul might have the odd idea that Brad's lovely cousin Rosamond had the most to lose or gain by David's arrival," Jim said dead-pan, seating himself on the step and stretching his long legs out into the sun. "But of course in her case it's only a trifling matter of marrying David or not."

I'd met Rosamond less than forty-eight hours ago. Nevertheless I stood my ground. "Well, comparatively, I'll bet it is a trifling matter. Rosamond can keep right on with what seems to be a very satisfactory way of life, even if the marriage doesn't come through. But Brad and Mary will literally be at the end of their rope."

Jim took his time lighting a cigarette, pushing the burnt kitchen match deep into the earth, before he spoke. I had a feeling he had intended to say more, changed his mind. "I'm afraid you're right," he reluctantly agreed. "If they lose this place, they lose everything."

And lose it they would, unless substantial financial aid were forthcoming between now, early in August, and October first, when their option to buy the property expired.

Mary and Brad themselves had told us this much.

Of the ill luck that hitherto had attended their twenty years of marriage, they had said nothing. It was, however, common knowledge. We'd heard their story from a half dozen outsiders, and although there was sharp variation in interpretation, the factual outlines had not materially differed.

Mary, born and brought up out here in Jackson Hole, had taken a job as waitress at a large and fashionable dude ranch the summer she was eighteen. Ambitious to enter the state university in September, her partisans said; ambitious to marry a rich dude, her detractors maintained. In any event, before September came, she'd achieved headline notoriety as the star witness in a trial for manslaughter.

Bradford Sloan, Princeton junior; in journalese the scion of a wealthy Eastern family, had been accused and all but convicted of the fatal shooting of a cowboy named Naboth Bishop, whose body had been found near the river road the morning after a ranch party. A dance that had ended in a brawl, due to the quality and quantity of raw moonshine that had been consumed.

One of the younger ranch hands had informed the sheriff that Bradford Sloan had left the dance floor swearing he'd find Naboth and kill him. Other witnesses, when subpoenaed, had perforce corroborated this testimony. Brad himself disclaimed all memory of his movements during the crucial hours. He had blacked out, he said.

It was then, after a defense attorney had been engaged on his behalf and a psychiatrist summoned, that Mary had come forward.

She had solemnly sworn and deposed that she had intercepted Brad outside the dance hall and recognizing his condition, had gone with him to his cabin, where she had spent the entire night. People had been known to die of raw moonshine, so she had stayed on guard until late morning.

Due to her unshakable testimony, Brad had been acquitted. He and Mary had been married at once. The price of her testimony, one faction heatedly argued to this very day. If so, it had proved Dead Sea fruit.

Brad was not the scion of a wealthy family. Orphaned at an early age, he'd been brought up among rich relatives; all of whom, with but one notable exception, had disowned him after marriage. A remittance man with the unprincely remittance of forty-five dollars a month from a trust fund, possessing no skill save riding, he had eked out a meager living by breeding and training horses on land Mary's father had homesteaded.

Then last autumn, on his fortieth birthday, the trust was dissolved, the corpus paid him outright. His long-cherished hope of owning a dude ranch seemed within his grasp. Optimistically he had entered into a short-term purchase agreement for this ideally situated but badly run-down luxurious private ranch, intending to do the major part of the work of restoring it himself. Scarcely had he moved here with his wife and daughter, however, when he'd been thrown by a recalcitrant colt, and suffered a severe heart attack. From that time forward all physical exertion was forbidden him.

He had been forced to hire professional labor for the requisite renovations at a cost that had eaten so deeply into his funds as to wipe out the possibility of making even this first year's payment of capital and interest. Ironically, as a result of his extensive improvements, a cash offer for outright purchase of the property had been tendered the executor of the estate to which it belonged. An offer he was bound by law to accept if Brad failed to come through.

At this juncture, the sole blood relative who had championed Brad through thick and thin, his cousin Rosamond Conner, as resourceful as she was beautiful, had put both gifts to work in hatching a possible solution.

Deeply devoted though she was to Brad, and perhaps unable to rid herself of a measure of responsibility for his original disaster, since she had urged his joining her at the dude ranch where it had occurred, Rosamond could not directly provide the sizable sum required. A widow whose personal fortune had been dissipated by a ne'er-do-well husband, she now possessed small means beyond her salary as style consultant in an expensive Fifth Avenue shop. But indirectly, Rosamond might become the means of Brad's salvation.

It would be part and parcel of a radically new way of life for her. A way of life that in worldly terms would be the reverse of sacrifice. Yet one had only to look at her to realize she must have remained a widow solely from choice. And even now, with so extraordinarily advantageous a marriage in prospect, she had made conditions, refused to consider marriage except on her own terms.

The crucial question as to whether David Ferensen would decide to meet those terms, agree to those conditions, was one about which Jim refused to make even an educated guess.

I had closed my eyes against the noonday glare; I opened them to see Jim getting to his feet. Mary Sloan's briskly moving blue-jeaned figure was headed in our direction.

She seemed small indeed beside his tall figure. Her short fair hair, at its roots the ash blonde of mine, had been dried and bleached by perennial wind and sun, her skin weatherbeaten. She'd once been deemed the prettiest girl for miles around; all that remained was an air of indomitable valor. But though she now stood almost challengingly erect, the unwonted distress in her blue eyes warned of bad news.

She said without preliminaries, "Walt's brother turned up while you folks were out riding, to collect Walt's things. Seems Walt was hurt a lot worse than we thought. He's gone home to Idaho. No telling how long before he'll be able to come back to work."

"Oh, Mary!" I felt almost sorrier for her than for Walt. This was a blow that would have felled an ordinary mortal. Walt was called the wrangler; he might more aptly have been called the mainstay of the ranch, the indispensable factor.

Yesterday, Sunday, had been his day off. He'd stayed in Jackson Saturday night and presumably got into a fight, judging from the cautious report over the party-line telephone last evening to the effect that he was in the hospital but hoped to return today.

"Lord knows I could never substitute for him," Jim said, "but anything I can do to help out . . ."

"Thanks, Jim." It was all Mary said in words, but the pause before she spoke again was eloquent. "Brad's spent most of the morning down at the bunkhouse telephoning. Susan's ridden up to the Ranger station to see if they know of anyone. Trouble is, anybody worth his salt has got himself a job long before now."

She squared her shoulders. "Well, we'll manage somehow. And meanwhile Brad wants you to come over for a drink. Lunch may be late. You can have some milk to tide you over, Elizabeth. And Rosamond's opened her cache of fancy cheese."

"We'll be right over," Jim assured her.

"Personally, I could eat a bear," he said when Mary's staunch figure had disappeared. "But failing anything so substantial, I'm glad the lovely Rosamond is on the job; she'll be bound to produce something tasty."

I nodded absent-mindedly, without moving.

"Up and at 'em," Jim said, taking my hands to hoist me out of the long chair. "You've got a starved look yourself."

"I'm worried," I confessed when I was on my feet. "It seems so terrible, so unjust, that something else should have gone wrong. It's as if there was some evil genius—"

I stopped short, hearing an unwelcome inner voice that made a mockery of blind chance. "Character is Destiny."

"Listen, my darling," Jim's actual voice was saying. "If there's any practical thing we can do for Mary and Brad, we'll do it more than gladly. But don't, in the name of common sense, let yourself become emotionally involved in matters that are completely outside our control. We did, after all, come out here for a vacation. We left the babies with your parents so you could be free of all responsibility, and gain back some of those pounds you lost. Don't turn this into a busman's holiday."

"I won't," I promised. "You're right as rain." I meant it, too.

But after he had started toward the main cabin and I'd gone inside in search of lipstick vivid enough to match the candy stripe in my best new shirt, I knew I'd promised more than I could perform.

Outwardly I would be detached, of course.

This resolution, as a matter of record, I was to keep for all of twelve days. But whether I was wrong not to have broken it sooner is a question that even now sometimes jerks me awake in the night.

2

Ready to start out, I changed my course, having caught sight of our two neighbors and fellow New Yorkers, Kevin Greene, a recently licensed M.D., and his ten-year-old nephew, Johnny.

Their cabin and ours were the only ones located on this side of the main building, away from the river. A proximity greatly to my liking.

Kevin's greeting was blithe, for which I gave him high marks when I saw his swollen and blistered face, covered with yellow ointment. He'd lost his hat yesterday in the course of a long ride, and having the delicate skin that goes with carrot-red hair, the sun's rays at seven thousand feet had been merciless.

As we stopped to discuss the calamitous news about Walt, I gave Johnny even higher marks for stoicism. He was a manly little boy, and an attractive looking one, sun-browned almost to the color of his unruly brown hair. Justifiably he had idolized the wrangler, yet he only said, "Walt's brother took his dog along too. I guess he would have been lonely here without Walt."

Johnny's own loss would be irreplaceable, I thought. He was the only child on the ranch, due to a last-minute cancellation by the parents of twin boys his age. An unexpected contingency that had resulted in Jim's and my being here. David Ferensen, having learned from Rosamond of the vacancy and from Jim of the virus that had caused me to lose appreciable weight, had urged our coming. Up to now, Johnny had not missed the companionship of contemporaries; Walt, the finest kind of old-time Westerner, innately wise about the needs of city-bred boys brought up by widowed mothers, had taught Johnny to ride, to fish, to be at home in the natural world. Beyond this, Walt had hoped, before the summer ended, to have reconciled the boy to his mother's recent remarriage.

"If Walt had come back with us after the movie Saturday night," Johnny said presently, "I don't suppose he would have had the accident, do you, Mrs. Little?"

"No. I don't suppose he would," I said, turning now to leave.

But a month's wages had been burning a hole in Walt's pocket, and on Saturday nights Jackson was a lively place indeed. I'd been surprised that Walt had wasted time going to the early showing of a Grade B Western with us. Although once there, it had been a tossup as to whether he or Johnny had more zestfully enjoyed himself. Johnny had been breathless with excitement at the daredevil stunt riding; Walt had been doubled up with silent mirth.

"Used to know that Hollywood cowboy; dastardly wall-eyed jughead," he'd said with a glance at Johnny, on our way from the theater to the Wort Hotel to join forces with Brad and Rosamond, just arrived from New York. . . .

"I was about to send out a Saint Bernard," Jim said as I entered the spacious living room where he and Brad were alone.

Brad moved forward with the warmth of welcome that was second nature to him. Solidly built, dark of hair and complexion, with a singularly sweet smile, he somehow conveyed the impression of a country squire—an extremely hospitable country squire.

His true vocation is that of host, I thought, as he made a pleasant ceremony of handing me the glass of milk ready on the tray.

"Now sit down where I can look at you," he said. And when I was seated on the large chintz-covered sofa, he turned to Jim. "How did you ever manage to get a girl like this, a man who went to public school?"

We all laughed. Yet incomprehensible though it seemed, Brad had been genuinely surprised, if not shocked, at learning that Jim, born and brought up in Denver, had not attended either an eastern preparatory school or college but had gone directly from the University of Colorado to the Yale Law School. Because Brad's own career at Princeton had been disrupted, he gave it scant mention. But that he'd been a Groton boy, we'd learned within the first hour of our acquaintance.

If our acquaintance had ended with that first hour, I'd have misjudged him sorely. For during these intervening two weeks he had revealed in deeds a warmth and sweetness of nature that more than counterbalanced his verbal foibles. There was not a selfish bone in his body. Nor had I ever heard him utter a word of complaint, although the physical inactivity forced upon him by what he called his old ticker, must be hell for a man of forty accustomed all his life to the most strenuous outdoor exercise.

Intellectual giant he was not, but in view of his present ignominious situation, his boasting of the past seemed a wholly forgivable form of whistling in the dark.

Today, I thought, he must be almost sick with anxiety about the defection of the wrangler, on whom so much depended. That Brad could keep up a flow of cheerful small talk, no matter how absurd intrinsically or how besprinkled with clichés, won my unqualified respect.

Mary came in carrying a carton of cigarettes, just as he was saying, as he invariably said when raising his prescribed glass of Scotch and water, "This is purely medicinal."

He paused before tasting it, turned to his wife. "Sure you won't join us, Mary?"

On the surface it was a courteous query, even if rhetorical, since Mary never drank hard liquor. Yet by its formal courtesy it seemed to mark the cleavage between them that Rosamond's presence had induced. I'd seen no sign of it during those relaxed unclouded days before she had appeared. Indeed I'd thought that Brad and Mary, despite the difference in their respective early backgrounds, despite the tragic circumstances surrounding their marriage itself, had proved excellently suited to each other.

Yet even this mere day and a half since Rosamond's appearance had wrought a change in them both. Never loquacious, Mary had become laconic, unduly sparing of words, and occasionally unduly defensive in such words as she did utter.

In answer to Brad's question now she merely shook her head, while her small rough hands busied themselves filling the several cigarette boxes.

The door into the dining room creaked. Brad glanced around, and a smile lighted his face. A special smile, compounded of pride and affection and an increased sense of his own worth.

I did not need to look up to know it was his cousin Rosamond who'd come in.

Nor, knowing the facts, could I wonder at the niche she occupied in his heart. Rosamond had come out here to visit him every summer during these past twenty years, when Brad had been cast off as the black sheep by the rest of his family in the East. And up to this current summer

Rosamond's visits had necessitated her adjusting herself to living conditions scarcely less primitive than the pioneers'.

Even had she been a plain woman, Brad would have had ample cause for pride. And Rosamond was the reverse of plain.

Rosamond was one of the few authentic beauties I've ever seen. It was not only a matter of her beautiful face, framed by black hair smoothly knotted at the base of her slender neck, but the effect of her total being, her exquisitely proportioned figure, her voice, her clothes.

She wore today what at first glance seemed the regulation outfit; in point of fact, however, her blue jeans and shell-pink linen shirt had been made to measure in the New York establishment where she reigned as arbiter of correct feminine attire for each and every sport in which the rich and fashionable indulged.

Her name was one with which to conjure in circles such as those. So great was her renown as a horsewoman, it had penetrated even my quite different orbit; although naturally I'd not known until Brad told me, that she'd won her first blue ribbon when she was only six. At a horse show in Newport, he'd not failed to add. Nor had he failed to mention her subsequent prowess in the hunting fields of various countries, including Ireland. Where, unfortunately, he'd said in a gruff parenthesis, she'd met and married a man named Conner. "A handsome devil and a crack rider, by all reports, but a total loss otherwise. He ran through all her money before his neck was broken in a steeplechase."

From another, less prejudiced, source I'd heard that the late Mr. Conner had been a jockey. "And not a gentleman jockey. His fingernails were always dirty and he was never known to wear a clean shirt."

It was not surprising she had remained so long a widow, or that her head now ruled her heart when it came to matrimony, I reflected, my judgment softened by the substantial canapés of smoked cheese she was proffering.

And she certainly should be able to make her own terms, I thought further, after she had seated herself beside Brad on the long fire bench. Her coloring alone merited Jim's adjective of lovely. Her eyes, dark-lashed, were the blue of blue violets. Fair-skinned, careful always to protect her complexion from the direct rays of the sun, her cheeks were the delicate shell-pink of her high-collared linen shirt

She addressed Mary, who had glanced out at the road. "'Are they coming, sister Anne?'"

"No," Mary said flatly, and the contrast to Rosamond's charming voice was marked. "We'll hear the car before it's in sight."

"Where's our daughter Susan?" Brad wanted to know.

"If she's back, I suppose she's primping."

"An excellent idea."

Whether meant as a hint to Mary, she obviously interpreted it in such light. Her hand flew to her streaked blonde hair. There was such combativeness in the stance of her small erect figure, I expected her to say, as she'd said to me when asking if I'd do an errand for her in town this afternoon, "I've been so all-fired busy getting ready for the new dudes I've let my hair get like straw."

She actually said, "Oh, well, at my age, what difference does it make?"

If her intention had been to strike at Rosamond, some six years her senior, it left Rosamond the easy victor. Now that I stopped to think of it, she looked decidedly younger than poor Mary. More significant, this was the first time I had stopped to think of it. Chronologically Rosamond might be almost forty-five, but in her presence every other female was diminished.

This went even for eighteen-year-old Susan, now rushing in, her fresh pretty face glowing with excitement, her brown eyes shining. And one corner of her red-and-white checked shirttail hanging out over her blue jeans. "A wrangler is on his way to apply for Walt's place!"

It was Rosamond, not her father or her mother, to whom she spoke, Rosamond who answered. "You've saved the day. However did you do it?"

"I didn't, really," Susan said honestly. "I mean I just told everybody I saw that we desperately needed someone, and when I got home just now I heard the telephone ringing in Walt's cabin and the operator said she'd been trying to get us and someone was coming over in a little while who has experience in handling dudes."

"What's his name?" Mary asked.

But her daughter had paused not only for breath, she'd made straight for the plate of cheese and crackers. "Don't know," she said, scarcely intelligibly. "Has his own horse, though."

Rosamond raised a slim admonishing hand. "A pretty girl has pretty manners."

"You're quoting that French governess of yours, Madame Picard," Brad said, apparently unable to resist any opportunity for nostalgic reminiscences about the early days shared with Rosamond. The happiest years of his life seemed to have been the span between the ages of five and eleven when he'd been a member of her household in the Virginia hunting country. A household disrupted by divorce. Rosamond, also an only child, had been free of all restriction save that imposed by the oft-mentioned Madame Picard.

Mary said dryly, "'Handsome is as handsome does' is the way it went in Wyoming."

"In Colorado too," Jim said, and I could have embraced him.

"'Beauty is only skin deep' they taught us in Medical School."

I turned my head, recognizing Kevin's voice, then joined in the shout of mirth. He looked like a red-haired zombie, his face swathed in gauze, only his mouth and bright eyes visible.

"Look, Mary," he said, having declined a drink, "I don't want to scare the wits out of the new dudes, so couldn't Johnny and I eat our lunch in the kitchen? Mrs. Pritchett won't mind. She has a soft spot for that kid nephew of mine."

"You bet."

Mary was halfway across the room when Brad's voice stopped her. "They can't eat in the kitchen!"

She wheeled around; with palpable effort tightly closed her lips.

Rosamond came to the rescue. "Brad, you old Tory, you're living in a world that's gone forever. Kevin's solution is perfect." She accorded the lanky young doctor a smile of approval. "Mrs. Pritchett is a grand old party; you'll probably have more fun than we will."

Brad capitulated. But he was still frowning after Mary and Kevin had disappeared, and Susan had picked up a bottle of Coke and flown off to change. "Damn it all, I'd supposed we would live like civilized people, once we were in this place."

"I hardly think David Ferensen would regard Kevin's face as a particularly civilized sight at his first meal here," Rosamond said quietly, unmistakably the older cousin now. "Or have great faith in him as the ranch physician."

Brad flushed. After a second he said, "You're right as usual, Rosie. I keep forgetting I've become an innkeeper. Having Elizabeth and Jim here is just like entertaining friends. . . . Let me freshen your drink, Jim."

"Make it light, or I'll fall asleep before David gets here."

Rosamond glanced up at Jim. "You've no real idea of what his daughter's like, have you?"

Since she'd asked the same question yesterday, its repetition betrayed a nervousness that surprised me, coming from her, natural though it would have been on the part of the average woman about to meet for the first time a girl of nineteen whose stepmother she might become.

"Not the foggiest idea," Jim said just as noncommittally as before, although going into more detail now. "The last time I went out to Ohio to see David we polished off our business at the plant earlier than expected, so he took me to the house for a drink. We stayed only a few minutes. I hardly said two words to Dorothy. I got the impression that she was shy; very young for her years, compared to Susan, for instance."

Over his glass Jim's eyes met mine. He had told me, but had no intention of telling Rosamond, that rarely had he felt more uncomfortable than during those few minutes at the house. A huge old-fashioned mansion on a hilltop overlooking the extensive buildings in the valley where the pottery was made, it was the home of David's mother-in-law, as that domineering old lady had made all too clear.

She had treated Dorothy as if she were a helpless small child and David as if he were still the teen-age farm boy who'd taken a job as day laborer in the plant. Although even by the time he'd married her daughter, dead now for many years, he'd achieved a white-collar job in the department of design.

During the intervening period he'd rescued the business from near bankruptcy, and built it up to such awesome prosperity he could now sell it on terms that would enable him to retire with a fortune of dazzling proportions.

And sell it he must, of course, if he were to marry Rosamond.

They had met within a matter of months, through a business acquaintance of David's in New York. David had instantly been bowled over.

How Rosamond had felt I could judge only on the basis of the common-sense stipulations she had made condition to agreeing to marry him, the levelheaded blueprint for their shared future, if any.

The first step would be David's removing himself, root and branch, from Ohio. New York would become headquarters, from which to launch David's daughter and Rosamond's young cousin Susan. A country place might be acquired in one or another of the hunting communities where Rosamond now spent the weekends exercising her friends' horses.

But no matter what they might do the rest of the year, they would spend the major part of every summer right here, in this precise spot.

Which would provide the justification for David's financing the ranch project.

And that was all that concerned me about either David Ferensen or Rosamond at that moment when the musical notes of an automobile horn catapulted us from our seats.

3

Mary emerged from the kitchen wing and joined Rosamond and Brad near the driveway just as the long, powerful tan convertible came to a stop.

The first passenger to alight was a tall slender girl with sandy hair, wearing blue sunglasses. Her beige dress understandably was wilted and she looked pale, as newcomers usually did.

At first glance, there seemed an absurdly strong family resemblance between her and the tall slenderly built man with sandy hair who stepped down at her heels. He too was somewhat disheveled. He too wore blue sunglasses.

Instantly he whipped them off, and his delight in being here was manifest. It was a second before he could tear his gaze from Rosamond's beautiful face or find his voice. "This is my daughter Dorothy," he said then. "Dorothy, this is Mrs. Conner, you've heard so much about."

Fortunately for his state of exhilaration, he was immediately caught up in Brad's and Mary's welcome, prevented from observing the frigidity of his daughter's response to Rosamond.

Rosamond held out her hand, smiling enchantingly beneath the wide-brimmed black hat she'd paused to put on before coming outdoors. Dorothy, a half head taller, made no pretense of smiling. Her lips were set in a tight compressed line.

David had caught sight of Jim's tall figure; the warmth of his liking was unmistakable. A warmth that extended to me by proxy.

I found myself thinking with surprise as we shook hands, "Why, he's nice! He's one of the nicest men I've ever met."

There was something about his eyes, some indefinable quality deeper than candor, that swept away my every reservation. Here was a man all of a piece; unworldly, unsophisticated, and incapable of pretense or of guile.

Susan came flying around the corner, prettier than I'd ever seen her in a sky-blue shirt, her short curling brown hair glistening in the sun. She made straight for Dorothy. "Golly, I'm glad you're here!" she said exuberantly. "It's absolutely wonderful."

There was no answering enthusiasm on Dorothy's part. The contrast between the two, within a year of the same age, was pitiable. Not only because of Susan's glowing color and vitality, but because she was outgoing by temperament, ready to like everyone, taking for granted she'd be liked in return. She had been counting the days until Dorothy's arrival, looking forward joyfully to the companionship of another girl.

In her lack of self-consciousness she was slow now to perceive that her friendly overtures were being deliberately rejected. Her initial reaction of disbelief was transparent, as was the bewildered hurt look in her deep-set brown eyes as she abruptly turned away, her cheeks crimson.

The remaining member of the party, Amos Landry, had descended without haste or eagerness from the car. Although a well built, brown-haired man of twenty-three or so, he was no Adonis. Nor was his light summer suit any less rumpled and travel-worn than his companions'.

Nevertheless he displayed such overweening self-confidence, an uninformed onlooker would have assumed it was he who was the tycoon, not the secretary.

Then as I heard him speak, the answer was obvious. At least to my insular New York ears, his way of speaking in itself conveyed an indefinable assumption of superiority: it was the quintessence of the loftiest Boston-Harvard manner.

Brad's recognition was as immediate as mine, even if markedly different in kind. He said with the eagerness of an exile in an alien land who prays he may have discovered a compatriot, "Did you by any chance go to Groton? It was my school."

Plainly this was the last question Amos Landry had expected to have fired at him on arrival in the great open spaces. His astonishment was unconcealed. Yes, he had happened to go to Groton, he said; then went quickly on to ask whether his saddle had arrived.

"It arrived all right," Susan said with an unnatural brittle laugh. "But we didn't take it out of its packing case; you can't use an eastern saddle on these horses. They aren't broken to it."

"That wouldn't faze Amos Landry," Rosamond said, coming forward and introducing herself to him. "David's told me how superbly you ride. You'll be much more comfortable out here in a Western saddle, though. I know I am."

"That settles it then," he said matter-of-factly. "I saw you perform at the New York Horse Show last fall."

Rosamond thanked him with a smile. Before moving off she gave her young cousin Susan a sidewise warning glance.

It went unheeded. Susan, as yet a child of nature, having been rebuffed by Dorothy, had no intention of trying to endear herself to the other young stranger.

"I suppose you'll try to post to a trot, too," she said with disdain.

"Just now," the Bostonian retorted coolly, winning the final round, "I'm more interested in washing up."

Dorothy moved quickly toward the car when Brad suggested they drive over to their cabins. He had turned to open the door of the convertible when young Johnny came streaking out of the main cabin.

"Lookit!" he cried, beside himself with excitement. "Lookit who's coming!"

He pointed down the road, a half-eaten chunk of coconut cake dropping unnoticed into the grass.

It was a small boy's dream of glory that met my gaze.

Advancing toward us was a high-stepping black horse, silver trappings glistening in the sun, ridden by a man picturesquely garbed in wide black hat, jade-green shirt, and black silk scarf tied high around his throat.

Still some distance away, the horse suddenly reared. For a seeming eternity horse and rider, defying the laws of gravity, remained silhouetted almost perpendicularly against the clear blue sky.

As theatrically effective a performance as if rehearsed endlessly before cameras.

And so it had been, I realized, breathing again as the forelegs came down onto solid earth. I'd seen the same horse, the same handsome rider, in the Grade B Western movie two nights ago.

"So that's the new wrangler," Susan said.

It seemed unthinkable; this romantic figure belonged solely to the world of make-believe. One black-gauntleted hand upraised in salutation, he maneuvered the spirited horse over to the hitching rail.

"God Almighty!" Brad exclaimed. "It's Spike Noland."

A small choked sound drew my attention to Mary. Then quickly I looked away; the blood seemed to have drained from her face.

David Ferensen was standing well on the outskirts of the group; his excitement almost equaled young Johnny's. "This is better than a circus, isn't it?" he said, smiling down at the child.

"I think he's even better than Roy Rogers!" was the accolade.

Even on foot, Spike Noland was an impressive figure, which is more than can be said of most horsemen. Compactly built rather than rangy, there was the suggestion of pantherlike ease in his walk. Sweeping off his hat, he smiled at the assemblage as a whole, his teeth noticeably white against the deep sun bronze of his skin. His hair was dark, with the hint of a wave.

It was toward Brad he advanced, removing his glove and holding out his hand. "Howdy, Mr. Sloan."

His agreeably deep drawling voice showed signs of professional training, as did his every gesture. I bit my lip as he added, departing from the script, "Long time no see."

"Twenty years," Brad said, his tone as brusque as his brief handclasp.

Mary stepped forward belligerently, a formidable figure despite her physical smallness.

"You can just get back on your horse, Spike Noland, and ride away."

"Well, now, I don't hold any hard feelings," he said, his drawl even more pronounced, "I'm ready to let bygones be bygones. I heard you folks needed someone experienced to help you out and I happened to be in the neighborhood. Before I went to the Coast I worked on a dude ranch near Reno. Not meaning to blow my own horn, but I appeared to give satisfaction."

I'll bet you did, I thought. If I'd ever seen the answer to an unhappy matron's prayer . . .

"Save your breath," Mary said. "We don't want you here and that's all there is to it."

Johnny's lip quivered. "Ah, gee, Mrs. Sloan!"

Brad glanced at Johnny, then at David Ferensen. He did not glance at Mary. Yet there was acute mindfulness of her in the bravado with which he turned to Spike Noland. "If you'll work for the going wage, and do your own cooking, it's a deal."

"It's a deal." Spike's teeth flashed as he smiled. "I've got my trailer parked over to Moose; I can fetch my duds and be back right away."

"Leave the trailer at Moose. There's a jeep at the bunkhouse you can use."

"Okie-doke." Spike seemed ready to leave. Then he spied Rosamond, who'd moved to the far edge of the semicircle as if to disassociate herself completely from the proceedings. "Why, Mis' Conner!" he said, taking a tentative step in her direction.

Pretending not to see or hear him, Rosamond bent over and busied herself in picking up the cake and every scattered crumb Johnny had let fall into the grass.

From her it was as telling and as personal as Mary's vocal rejection of Spike. For one thing, Rosamond's manners were of the school that excluded unintentional rudeness. For another, I'd witnessed her freemasonry with Walt, and with far rougher and less well-educated cowboys, at the hotel in Jackson Saturday evening; her easy camaraderie contrasting sharply with the coolness she'd displayed toward run-of-the-mill Eastern tourists who'd come out on the train with her. No, her attitude now could not be put down to conventional snobbery; it had to tie up with Spike as an individual.

David Ferensen, who naturally had no way of knowing all this, lost no time in cordially shaking Spike's hand. "And this is my daughter," he said then.

"Mighty pleased to meet you—" Spike looked at Dorothy a second longer than convention demanded. And under that look, she flushed.

Nor did I blame her, when in turn I was subjected to the lingering intimate gaze of those velvety dark eyes.

That our Paradise was now complete with serpent, I could not doubt. Despite his absurd affectations, Spike Noland possessed an elemental quality of attraction that was almost palpable.

Susan was immune to it. She alone seemed genuinely indifferent to everything about Spike except his magnificent steed. What was the horse's name? she asked.

Diamond, he told her; and placing his wide black hat jauntily on his handsome head, he paused only long enough to say, "Better put the show on the road," before moving toward the hitching rail.

With his departure, there was a general dispersal. When everyone else had gone, Kevin joined Jim and me on the lawn. From the kitchen window he'd enjoyed a splendid view. He'd also enjoyed the benefit of Mrs. Pritchett's running commentary.

Mrs. Pritchett, an expert laundress and cleaning woman, drove over early every morning in an ancient Ford and returned every evening to her married daughter's home near the Gros Ventre. She described herself as the lady help. Whether with equal accuracy she could be termed a gossip was a moot point. I took the negative side; there was no grain of malice in her hundred and sixty-odd pounds.

She couldn't believe her eyes, so Kevin now reported, when Spike Noland had ridden up. He had the nerve of a brass monkey.

"She called the turn there," Jim said. "He gave us a one man show: 'Don Juan of the Sagebrush.' He's forty if he's a day, Kevin; getting a bit heavy, which may be why he's washed up on the screen. And his teeth are capped."

"I was particularly taken with the cock-of-the-walk swagger," Kevin said, gingerly touching the gauze bandages over his inflamed forehead.

"He's a beautiful hunk of man," I declared, with difficulty keeping a straight face as I saw Jim's astonished stare. "An absolute dream boat." Then I spoiled it all by laughing.

He put his arm around my shoulders. "You had me worried for a moment; I was afraid you'd had a touch of the sun."

"I'm sorry I missed a close-up," Kevin said.

"You'll have plenty of time to make up for it," Jim said wryly. "He's been engaged as wrangler."

Kevin's amazement became ours when he told us what else Mrs. Pritchett had said.

It had been Spike Noland's testimony that had nearly sent Brad to the penitentiary.

4

Mrs. Pritchett herself materialized, her ample: form adorned in a beruffled red-dotted Swiss dress. I assumed she'd joined us to continue the story at first hand. Instead she said with unaccustomed gravity, "If you'd not mind getting your laundry together, Mrs. Little, I'd like to take it now. Lunch won't be ready for another thirty, forty minutes."

Not until we were inside the cabin, out of earshot of the men, did she say more.

Mary, it developed, had sent her out of the kitchen; Mary was slamming pots and pans around as if she'd gone plumb loco. "Never saw her carry on like this before. Sometimes I've thought it would do her good if she did break loose."

Silently I began counting the surprising number of shirts.

"It's one thing some people hold against her, that she always keeps a stiff upper lip," Mrs. Pritchett said, sorting the handkerchiefs into two piles. "But I guess she'd have to be made of stone to take this."

In addition to a cotton dress I produced two linen skirts, Jim having an unconquerable aversion to women wearing trousers save when the exigencies of ranch life demanded blue jeans.

"I don't think these will need any starch."

"Guess not." Absent-mindedly Mrs. Pritchett fingered the material, then her troubled eyes met mine.

"It don't seem right that Mr. Sloan should have hired that—that Spike Noland!" she burst out.

And now that she'd started, I doubted whether anything short of complete paralysis of the jaw could have stopped her.

Spike Noland, one of the hands employed at the dude ranch where the Sloans had met, had always been a troublemaker; and the mainmost trouble he'd made had been with the girls. In Mrs. Pritchett's opinion, he'd had it in for Mary, working there temporarily as waitress, because she'd not fallen for him. Maybe he'd had it in for Mr. Sloan, too, because in those days he'd been—well, standoffish, with the help. Now he was plain as an old shoe, she hastened to say in Brad's praise. But she still called him Mr. Sloan.

Naboth Bishop, the cowboy whose death was still unsolved, had got along all right with Mr. Sloan, though, until the fatal night of the dance, Mrs. Pritchett had been there herself, she'd been in charge of the ranch laundry that summer.

"Seemed like the devil got into Naboth Bishop. Or maybe it was the liquor. He could have had his pick of all the womenfolks, but no, he had to start pestering Mary. First time he ever had noticed her that way. Not that Mary had to play second fiddle to anybody in those days; she's gone off something terrible now but she was mighty pretty then, and she was pert and had a mind of her own. The men liked that. She was more popular than even the dude girls, except maybe Mrs. Conner, but then she's different. Anyway, Mary could have had lots of partners if it hadn't been for that crazy Naboth. He kept rough-shouldering them away soon as they'd danced a step or so with her. Mr. Sloan wasn't the only one by any manner of means.

"Trouble was, he went outside and got himself filled up on raw moonshine. Might just about as well of drunk poison."

When Brad had returned, unsteady on his feet, Naboth had disappeared. Brad had started in pursuit, declaring he'd find Naboth and blow his so-called brains out.

The phrase had an odd ring of authenticity, I thought uneasily; moreover, once Spike Noland had testified to Brad's using it, other bystanders, questioned under oath, had been forced to substantiate his testimony.

Mary, as I already knew, had sworn she had intercepted Brad as he left the dance hall, taken him to his cabin and remained there with him throughout the night.

What I had not known, until Mrs. Pritchett now told me, was that this alibi had not weighed too heavily with the jury, unofficially. Their almost unanimous off-the-record verdict had been that Brad had done the shooting while temporarily of unsound mind. They were more than glad officially to acquit him.

The man most of them would have liked to convict was Spike Noland. The informer was far from a popular figure in these parts, and he was a peculiarly unsavory specimen; avaricious, self-seeking, a born show-off. He'd been wise to decamp shortly after the trial had ended.

"Been married two, three times since then," Mrs. Pritchett said, adroitly bundling the small mountain of vari-colored clothes into a huge bath towel and knotting the corners. His last marriage had been to a movie actress he'd met in Reno, and through whom he'd got into that picture that was showing here last week.

Why he had suddenly reappeared in Jackson Hole was a mystery to her, Mrs. Pritchett confessed, pinning the list

I handed her onto the bath towel. That it was for no good reason, she'd bet her last cent. "But what really beats me is why Mr. Sloan should have hired him."

Since I had no answer to that, Mrs. Pritchett herself came up with one. "Might be he figured it would prove to everybody he was innocent all the time. That his conscience was clear.

"On the other hand," she said and frowned, "He could be planning to get his revenge."

As we started across the lawn, carrying the bundle between us, the sunlight seemed to dispel this morbid fancy.

"Plain truth of the matter is," she said with her more accustomed practicality, "Mr. Sloan had to hire him some wrangler or shut up shop. All in all, looks like he had his both feet on the ground."

She added challengingly, as if I'd been the person who'd questioned Brad's motives, "He's got all his eggs in the one basket. If he fails now, it will go mighty hard with him. Jobs are scarcer than hen's teeth out here, even for able-bodied men. And on account of Mr. Sloan's heart condition, he can't do any kind of real work. But given half a chance," she finished with unconscious irony, "he'll be a cracker-jack dude rancher."

This, at least, was incontrovertible, I thought, our paths diverging after the laundry was stowed in her car.

Brad's gift for making strangers feel at home had already been exercised to good effect on David Ferensen, I noted with vicarious satisfaction when we were presently seated at the refectory table in the dining room.

By this time my appetite had increased to such proportions, it was not until I'd eaten the green salad as well as two portions of both the beef ragout and the Spanish rice, that I again gave more than token attention to my fellow men. With the arrival of dessert I realized that Brad was having uphill work indeed with Dorothy Ferensen. He had devoted himself to her, asking the kind of questions about her trip that even the most painfully shy of newcomers could answer without effort, and in the process gradually thaw out.

Dorothy answered in jerky monosyllables. She did not thaw out. Shyness was not her mainmost trouble, I felt certain, having witnessed her coldness to Susan earlier, and observing now her hostile glance toward the other end of the long table, where her father, seated beside Rosamond, was obviously in a state of enthraldom.

Perhaps Dorothy's resentment was inevitable, I thought, more charitable in my judgment than when hunger had gnawed. Perhaps no girl of nineteen could fail to feel bitterly hostile to the idea of her father's falling in love. Unless the girl herself were to fall in love.

A solution that might have occurred to Dorothy's father; might account for his bringing young Amos Landry along, counting on propinquity to perform its reputed magic. If so, David should have chosen someone else, I thought, hearing Amos say in almost a travesty of Harvard superiority: "But the Tetons can't be compared, of course, to the Alps." There was a lad to whom propinquity would be no friend.

In his turn, if Amos were attracted to Dorothy, it must be as the boss's daughter. With her sunglasses removed, wearing another unbecoming dress a shade lighter than her sandy hair, she was as colorless in appearance as she was unresponsive in manner.

"No, but the Tetons have their own grandeur," Jim was saying. "And there's no town in all of Switzerland that I'd be willing to swap for the town of Jackson."

"We came through it," Amos said. "Full of characters supposed to represent he-men. It struck me as a Potemkin village."

Susan's eyes widened in bewilderment, as he'd probably intended they should.

"Wait until you see Jackson some Saturday night," I said, speaking only out of irritation, with no sense of prophecy, "you'll find there's nothing unreal about it."

David's attention having been momentarily deflected from Rosamond, he watched me with open astonishment as I helped myself bounteously from the bowl of ripe red strawberries, poured thick yellow cream over them and then took a slice of coconut cake.

"'It's the altitude,'" I said, quoting the familiar catch-all phrase. "You'll be a trencherman, too, in a few days."

"I'm afraid I'd also have to lop about twenty-five years off my life," he said with a smile I savored even more.

The smile vanished.

"I'll be fifty years old a week from Saturday," he said as if uttering aloud a portentous fact that he himself found hard to credit. "That's the final crossroads. From which there's no turning back."

The sudden embarrassed hush was in itself a reminder that age was not the test. David's crossroads would prove the crucial turning point for everyone seated at the board, outside of Jim and me.

In the silence Mrs. Pritchett's voice became audible from the kitchen. "Go on with you! I'm a grandmother now and proud of it."

A second later Spike Noland came in.

He'd exchanged his flamboyant attire for a serviceable plaid shirt and blue jeans; his manner had likewise become workmanlike, respectful. Having advanced directly toward Brad, he stood a little distance back, rolling the brim of a medium-sized tan Stetson between his two hands. "While you folks are all together, thought I'd best find out who's going riding this afternoon."

Brad took a roll call, starting with David, who shook his head. "No. I'll wait until tomorrow, thanks all the same."

"How about you, Amos?"

"I'd like to go out, later on. But not in a crowd." His clipped accent said for him, "Not with this mountebank."

"Elizabeth? . . . No, you and Jim are going to town." Brad turned to Spike. "No customers until tomorrow, then."

Spike took a step toward Dorothy. "How about this little lady?"

She crimsoned. I'd not supposed she had as much red blood in all her veins as flooded her slender face. "I—I don't know," she stammered, casting a look of appeal at her father.

"It might do you good, Dorothy," he said, "after sitting so long in the car."

Rosamond and Mary exchanged glances. Worlds apart they might be in all else, but on this subject they seemed in complete accord. The situation was extremely delicate; they could hardly tell David that the wrangler Brad had engaged was not a man with whom a young girl should be alone.

Rosamond resolved the dilemma with characteristic resourcefulness. "I've got to exercise my horse sometime today," she said. "And I suggest that you come along, Amos; this isn't country to ride alone in, certainly not until you've learned a little more about its particular hazards."

"Johnny's raring to go, too," Jim said.

"Reckon I've bought something." Spike's voice was soft, courteous, yet amusement glinted in his dark eyes. Apparently it fed his vanity to be considered dangerous.

"You go along with them, Susan," Brad said. "It takes about one experienced rider for each raw dude," he told the newcomers at large. "As my cousin said, the country around here has some danger spots." He looked again at Spike. "That goes for you, too; the Snake overflowed this spring, washed away the underpinnings of the bank beneath the old road."

"Much obliged for telling me. I'll be mighty careful," Spike answered, in a travesty of humility.

He's got his roles mixed up, I thought; he's playing Uncle Tom, not an honest-to-God cowboy, who would have covered the situation with a laconic, all-encompassing, "You bet."

In actual performance as a cowboy, however, Spike was shortly to convince me that unorthodox methods possessed a merit of their own.

5

Halfway between the garage and the corral, Jim shut off the engine of our rented coupé; the riders had not yet set forth, and some of the horses shied at cars.

On foot we proceeded to a little knoll at the fork of the dirt road, where Kevin was standing, his tall lanky figure topped by a farmer's straw hat that shaded his unbandaged though still swollen face.

"The great sportsman," he said, laughing as he held up the camera with which he took such excellent colored pictures.

"I thought that if . . . if the ranch deal goes through," he went on seriously, "Brad might use a scene like this in that brochure he spoke of. Don't you think it would be a good come-on, Elizabeth?"

"It ought to entice anyone," I declared. "In fact, if you'll let us take the film I'll have an enlarged copy made and framed."

Jim nodded. "It will be a cheery sight on a cold winter day in New York."

. . . I paused just now, a cold winter day in New York, to disinter that picture, destined never to be framed, never to be hung, never to be looked at without the rush of tears. Yet after my vision cleared, during the brief moment before I hastily reburied the picture, I could see the external charm we saw on that sunlit afternoon of early August.

The camera caught a seemingly cohesive, united group, including spectators. Mary and David Ferensen, together with Mrs. Pritchett, were standing on the porch of the comfortable three-roomed cabin known as the bunkhouse.

In the background, the snowy peak of the Grand Teton rose into a cloudless azure sky. In the foreground, Susan's shirt repeated this lovely blue. She was keeping a watchful eye on the ten-year-old Johnny, clad in a bright red sateen shirt, while he tightened the cinch of the gentle mare he regarded as his personal possession. In front of the big red barn, Amos, in riding breeches and boots and white polo shirt, was putting a roping saddle on the powerful dapple-grey, whose bridle Brad was holding.

Only Rosamond was mounted. A striking figure she was, too, wearing a straight-brimmed black hat and riding clothes the color of the buckskin horse she was forcing to stand quietly near the bunkhouse while she talked to David. Reassuring him, perhaps, about his daughter. Or perhaps merely diverting his attention so he would not feel apprehensive.

Dorothy, dressed as for a city riding academy in striped shirt, necktie, jodhpurs and small brown felt hat, was watching Spike Noland adjust the stirrups of the roan selected for her use.

The lens did not catch the next few active minutes but they registered indelibly on my mind. Spike was instructing Dorothy how to guard against accidents by mounting correctly. It looks like one easy fluid motion when the expert swings up into the saddle. But to the novice, I thought with a surge of fellow feeling, it represents a succession of seemingly impossible steps, starting with the initial need to face away from the horse's head.

Dorothy's first tentative efforts were awkward, flustered. Smilingly Spike encouraged her to try again. Courageously she did, despite the size of the audience. When at last she succeeded I wanted to cheer.

"She has stamina, that girl," Kevin said admiringly.

"She's not the only one."

Jim glanced at me. And at his smile I blushed, despite four years of marriage. For it had been he who'd taught me to ride, and I'd been so desperately in love I'd not had sense enough left to be afraid; I'd wanted only to find favor in his eyes.

But Dorothy couldn't be impelled by any such motive, I told myself as the cavalcade started out; Susan in the lead, Spike on his beautiful black horse bringing up the rear.

"I hope Kevin's face gets back to normal soon," I said a few moments later in the seclusion of the car. "Both as a human being and a doctor, he'd be just the person to straighten Dorothy out."

Jim concentrated on maneuvering the coupé off the side road and into the fairly steady stream of southbound traffic on the highway that led north to Yellowstone Park. "I'll bite," he said then, relaxed. "Why does Dorothy need to be straightened out?"

"That speaks for itself: even you got the cold shoulder from her."

Jim laughed. "I admit the poor kid's harder to talk to than anyone I ever tackled. And she certainly doesn't know how to fix herself up. But those are things the lovely Rosamond should be able to cure in two easy lessons."

That will be the day, I thought. I said, "What's the low-down on Amos? Is he a candidate for Dorothy's heart and hand?"

"I meant to ask him first thing. And I forgot."

Then Jim relented. "My hunch is that David wouldn't be sorry to have Amos in the family. Nor would that dreadful grandmother of Dorothy's. Amos is eligible as all get out. Good Boston family. Money too. What appeals to David is that Amos is genuinely interested in the plant. He took the job as David's secretary instead of going to the Harvard Business School, with the idea that he'd learn a lot more in a shorter time that way. He's more intelligent than he seems."

"That's damning him with faint praise."

"Oh, he was just showing off at lunch for Susan's benefit. It's an odd way some men have."

"An undergraduate's way. And Amos must be twenty-three or four."

"About twenty-four. He was in Korea for a couple of years. Actually it was while he was in Japan on leave that he became interested in pottery. Hence the job with David."

"'Potemkin village!'" I quoted indignantly, my prejudice against Amos returning in full force as we rounded the horseshoe bend in the highway and beheld in the valley between us and the distant wooded mountains, the scattered small buildings, most of them one story high, that comprised the town of Jackson, population circa one thousand.

"My favorite metropolis. Favorite shopping center. The stores even stay open here on Saturdays, instead of closing the way they do in New York in the summer. And where is there a finer hostelry than the Wort brothers'?

"It might save time," I added less lyrically, "if I went first to the Wort Hotel and put in the long-distance call to Connecticut."

"Just what I was thinking," Jim said. "Though it shouldn't be an all-day job, the way it is on our party line . . . or used to be."

His tone had changed. Nor was there a spark of amusement in his eyes as he turned toward me. "You aren't ever again to go down to the bunkhouse to telephone, Elizabeth."

It was a command. Never had he spoken to me with such finality. It moved me to say no less earnestly, "To tell the truth I wouldn't want to go down there now. There's something about Spike Noland . . ."

"Good girl!" Jim's hand closed over mine. "Give my congratulations to your revered parents together with my love. Meanwhile I'll polish off some of the other chores."

He'd polished off quite a number and was seated at the literally named Silver Dollar bar, when I emerged from the telephone booth.

Among other errands, he'd gone to the hospital to get Brad's prescription renewed, he told me after I'd finished a milk punch as well as a digest of my mother's rapturous account of our two young.

The doctor who took care of Brad's old ticker had also attended to Walt's injuries. Jim had therefore hoped some light might be thrown on the Saturday night fracas. The coincidence of Walt's being disabled at just the moment Spike had reappeared, presumably in search of a job as wrangler, seemed a little too pat.

The physician's attitude had been co-operative but his information, scant. He suspected a crooked poker game, for Walt had just escaped being fatally hurt by what were locally known as brass knucks; and he had refused to say where or how. Gambling was against the law in Wyoming, but far too deeply embedded in the mores to be uprooted by legal statute. What the statute had accomplished was the extinction of the honest game, leaving the field open to the depredations of sharpers. Walt might have been the victim of some such gang.

"It's not very conclusive," Jim said. "And I still think Spike's mixed up in it somehow. Brass knuckles are what I'd expect from that . . ."

With effort Jim dismissed the subject. "Well, this isn't buttering any parsnips. Now what have you got to do?

Rosamond asked me to get some new bridge cards and score pads. She brought Brad a thick volume of Goren. David is by way of being an expert."

While Jim went into the stationer's I went into Miss McClung's Beauty Salon with Mary's brief but eloquent list: blonde hair nets, hair brush, pomade for dry hair.

Wanting to deliver this package first of all, I moved straight from the garage toward the kitchen as soon as we returned. Mary was apt to be there at this hour, since she cooked all the meals, and the electric lights were on.

Yes, there she was, I saw as I neared the unshaded window. She was standing by the big coal range, stirring an iron soup kettle. Her head and torso were turned well away from the stove, however. She was talking, smiling, with unwonted animation for any day, let alone a day like this.

Involuntarily I paused. Her companion was none other than David Ferensen. Seated in a rocking chair he was busily and without question happily shelling peas.

The cycle had come full turn, I thought, amused and pleased and determined not to intrude on the homely cozy scene. David had been born and brought up on a farm; he fitted far more naturally into these surroundings than he ever would in Rosamond's fashionable milieu. He'd probably want to spend a lot of time out here in the future. Brad could get busy on his brochure right away.

Then as I neared Mary's and Brad's cabin, I ran into Susan.

Her arms were filled with bright shirts and slacks; she put her mother's parcel into a deep pocket of her jeans to deliver later. "Dad's resting now," she said, and turned to walk back with me toward my own quarters.

She had just come from Dorothy's cabin, she explained. Dorothy hadn't realized how cold the nights were here and had brought silk dresses to change into for supper. "So I took over all my best things," Susan said. "The ones Rosamond gave me. I told Dorothy she could have her choice, and welcome. She wouldn't even look at them. She—she almost slammed the door in my face—"

Despite the gathering dusk I could see the tears Susan was trying to blink back. It must have cost her dear to make this second effort at friendliness when she'd been so flatly snubbed before.

I repeated what Jim had told me about Dorothy's unfortunate bringing up by her grandmother, who'd wrapped her in cotton wool. I made every excuse I could except the one I suspected outweighed all the others: Dorothy's resentment of Rosamond. Susan, as Rosamond's relative and adorer, would be regarded with sharp disfavor on that score alone.

"Well, that's just too bad," Susan said satirically when I'd finished my expurgated speech. "But for all of me she can stay wrapped up in her cotton wool. Just because she's rich—"

The defiance vanished. There was something very touching in Susan's quiet summing up. "I'd thought it would be such fun when the new people came. And now I wish they hadn't come at all."

It was a wish I myself came close to echoing an hour later, entering the living room of the main cabin, aware of its markedly changed atmosphere, far preferring the casualness of the earlier days.

I could even have gone a step beyond Susan and not been sorry if Rosamond also had stayed away, I thought wryly, vexed with myself for being vexed by Jim's low whistle of admiration when Rosamond came forward.

6

"That's the most stunning getup I've ever seen," Jim told Rosamond, blithely oblivious of having told me a few minutes earlier that trousers in any form were an abomination on any woman.

It was a stunning getup: frontier pants and brief jacket of deep violet-blue corduroy worn over a high-throated white silk blouse. It was also exceedingly becoming, deepening to violet the blue of Rosamond's dark-lashed eyes, emphasizing the fairness of her complexion, setting off her slim perfect figure.

Withal, there was an air of elegance from the crown of her satin-smooth black hair to the tips of her blue sandals, that reduced my yellow tweed skirt and cashmere pullover to the level of a sensible golfing outfit.

As for Dorothy Ferensen, who came in at our heels, her worst enemy might have chosen the tan slacks and cardigan that made her seem a dreary monochrome, save for the unbecoming cerise of her lipstick.

"I hope you're not stiff after your ride?" Rosamond asked with a solicitous smile.

"Not a bit," Dorothy said curtly. Ignoring the chair Brad pushed forward, she picked up a New York newspaper from the long table, carried it over to the far end of the room, and seated herself beside a reading lamp.

Brad glanced meaningly at Susan. Susan, her cheeks the scarlet of her fireman-red flannel shirt, shook her head of shining brown curls in a violent "No!" with more than ample justification. The newspaper in which Dorothy was pretending absorbed interest had been dated days before she left Ohio; Brad devoured each issue down to the very advertisements, before bringing it over here. What Dorothy patently desired to accomplish was isolation from the group around the blazing log fire.

She certainly doesn't take after her father, I thought as the dining-room door swung open and David came in carrying a large tray of drinks. To be sure he too was tall and slender and his hair was sandy in color; he presented an almost rustic appearance in a dark flannel shirt and Levi's. But he was surcharged with friendliness, he was buoyant.

He chuckled when Amos, arriving from outside, dressed as if he were still in Massachusetts in grey flannels and tweed jacket, moved quickly over to try to take the tray.

"No, you don't, my boy. I'm more accustomed to this kind of work than you—"

David stopped quite still, having caught sight of Rosamond.

"You . . . you ought to have your portrait painted in that costume," he said after a prolonged silence.

The way in which he looked at her, as if she were the most exquisite of museum pieces, reminded me that in his own field he was himself an artist.

He was also a man of great good will, I realized when he turned with a smile to Mary, who'd come in while he was placing the tray on its accustomed table.

"You didn't put any tomatoes in our minestrone behind my back, did you?"

"Wait and see," she said with an answering smile.

She'd not had time to do anything to her brittle sun-bleached light hair; the most that could be said for her white shirt and faded jeans was that they were clean. Nevertheless no one would think of pitying her; self-respect was manifest in the erectness with which she carried herself, in the gallant tilt of her chin.

About to sit down, doubtless for the first time in many hours, she noticed Dorothy, and hesitated, plainly torn between a sense of duty and desire to have a moment free from duty.

It was no lofty motive that prompted me to resolve the dilemma; the reason I gave was true; the fire was too warm for comfort, dressed as I was with the temperature of the dining room in mind.

It was cooler in every sense at Dorothy's end of the room. She put down the newspaper without any discernible enthusiasm when I seated myself beside her. But where Brad and Jim and Susan had all failed, I could cherish no illusions of grandeur about succeeding. A few platitudes couldn't do either of us any harm, though.

"The first day out here seems very strange; at least to me it did," I began. "It's partly the much talked of altitude."

Vastly complicated in her case by the shock of Rosamond's beauty, I suspected. Even an attractive girl might well quail before the competition so alluring a stepmother would offer. And no one could call this colorless girl attractive.

Her features were all right. And although her hair was cut too short for her slender face, it possessed a natural wave that made it spring crisply back from her forehead. Jim had been right in saying Rosamond could improve Dorothy's appearance in two easy lessons. Even I could.

As for Dorothy's apathy, however, it would take an earthquake. . . .

It took only the arrival of a ten-year-old boy, dark hair slicked down with water, tanned cheeks scrubbed and shining, wearing a grass-green sateen shirt, topped by a leather waistcoat.

Johnny made a beeline for this corner. Rosamond had suggested yesterday that the cocktail session was not the most appropriate place for children; this was not, however, Johnny's sole reason for taking refuge here.

He and Dorothy had already struck up an alliance in the course of the afternoon's ride. A ride they had manifestly enjoyed.

"And you know something?" Johnny looked up at me to say, "She was *good!*"

Despite the unconcealed surprise with which he delivered this opinion, it cracked the shell of Dorothy's resistance. She became almost vivacious as they exchanged notes across me about the expedition.

Oh, the poor wretched creature! I thought, not wanting to feel sorry for her, yet unable not to. I'd been ignoring the self-evident principle that it is the unlovely, the unattractive, who thirst most avidly for praise. Even the compliment of this small boy was causing Dorothy, if not exactly to blossom, at least to shed her prickliest thorns.

With Johnny she was not on the defensive; she became her natural self. A markedly immature self compared to most girls of nineteen. She'd been having riding lessons at home these past few months, she said.

"My father's recently become interested in horses." There was sarcasm in her tone and the accompanying sniff, as she glanced in Rosamond's direction, but it was childish sarcasm, of the kind Johnny himself might have employed. Although to do Johnny justice, he had taken refuge in manly silence upon learning of his mother's remarriage.

He and Dorothy had more in common than they might realize. Each one was in a way a misfit here. Each one had to face the bitterly unwelcome prospect of a step-parent.

In Johnny's case, there was the addition of a six-year-old stepsister, as yet unseen, but already hated.

With the exception in Johnny's favor of his stoicism, he and Dorothy were about the same mental age, I decided, preparing to move back to the adult group even if I roasted, when Johnny began describing in painstaking detail the Western movie in which Spike had appeared.

The front door opened while I was crossing toward the fire. Kevin's carrot-red head appeared.

David and he were already acquainted, it developed. "We had a nice little visit this afternoon," David said. "But I don't think you've met my daughter."

As he steered the tall young doctor toward Dorothy, Jim looked at me and grinned. "You needn't worry," I answered silently. "I wouldn't want to make a match there; I'm much too fond of Kevin."

Viewed solely as a public service, however, it was a boon to have Kevin's gay good humor exerted on Dorothy's behalf, to have him presently seat himself beside her at the dinner table, Johnny on her other side. The result was a general air of relaxation around the board, a genial house-party atmosphere with Brad the most charming of hosts, entertaining chosen friends on his ancestral acres.

Completely the country squire, he said rather grandly at the conclusion of the excellent meal his wife had cooked, "We'll have coffee in the other room."

"So that Mrs. Pritchett can clear off the dishes and get home," Mary somewhat marred the effect by adding.

Fresh logs had been put on the living-room fire, the cocktail things removed. Mrs. Pritchett had entered wholeheartedly into the new regime; the coffee service was in readiness in front of the most regal of the high-backed leather chairs.

"You pour it, will you, Rosamond?" Mary asked, and I would have supposed her mindful only of the incongruous effect her own workaday figure would present, had she not turned to David. "I want to get your oatmeal started."

There was more than one way to a man's heart, his swift smile of appreciation reminded me. "I seem to have developed some queer digestive kink," he said rather shamefacedly when we were seated together on a small sofa apart from the others and he was trying surreptitiously to down a yellow capsule. "Up to a few months ago I could eat nails. There's nothing organically wrong that any doctor can discover."

It had been only a matter of months since he'd met Rosamond, I recalled, and proceeded with my diagnosis. Even before I'd heard Kevin discuss psychosomatic medicine I'd discovered the inextricable connection between the nervous system and the powers of digestion. David was torn by conflicting emotions, pulled two ways. He must have some powerful reason for postponing his decision about selling the plant. Some reason rooted in his conscience. Certainly he was head over heels in love with Rosamond.

I glanced across the room at Dorothy. She looked almost pretty, transformed by the smile that lighted her face. A shy smile, yet one of unalloyed delight.

Kevin was standing in front of her, holding out sugar and cream. I took for granted that it was he who by some unexpected power of fascination had wrought this minor miracle.

I felt as if a sandbag had hit me on the head—or should have hit me—when I heard Spike Noland's soft drawl, realized Dorothy had been smiling at him.

"Good evening, folks."

Again in gala attire, wickedly handsome in a wine-red shirt with an artfully tied silk scarf, Spike now advanced toward Brad, carrying a guitar.

"Thought maybe you'd like a few songs with your coffee, Mr. Sloan. But if not, just say the word."

Brad's dark eyes narrowed almost to pin points. His ruddy face flushed cholerically. "We have the bridge table set up," he managed to say, making it a dismissal.

David leaned forward. "So far as I'm concerned, I'd far prefer a little music." He looked up at Spike. "Can you sing 'Give Me My Boots and Saddle'?"

"Yes, sir, I sure can."

And he sure could.

There was no song anyone was subsequently to name that he did not know. His voice was not of concert caliber, perhaps, but it wove a spell. At once warm and pleasing to the ear, it possessed an oddly poignant quality that moved me almost unbearably.

Nor was I the only person to be moved, I found.

Mary had not rejoined us. Amos, having learned that the only telephone on the ranch, and that a busy party-line affair, was located in the bunkhouse, had seized the opportunity of its being untenanted to put in a long-distance call. "I suppose you want to let your family know the Indians haven't scalped you yet," Susan had said, but at her father's request she had gone along as guide.

Before Spike had settled himself and his guitar on the long bench facing the semicircle made by the sofas and easy chairs, Brad had switched off all the lamps. The sole light came from the open fire behind our picturesque minstrel, and it was so faint as to leave the rest of us in obscurity. Obscurity that I for one found merciful, after I had unwisely asked for that most desolating of Western ballads, "Down in the Valley."

By the end of the first stanza there was a lump in my throat. It grew to painful proportions as Spike's poignant golden voice went on.

> *If you don't love me,*
> *Love who you please,*

Put your arms 'round me,
Give my heart ease

Give my heart ease, love . . .

A log crashed in two; bright flames shot up. In that instant's illumination Rosamond's face sprang at me, so to speak. She was staring into the fire, one hand clenched into a fist, pressed against her cheek. Above it a tear glistened.

Until now I'd not believed her capable of genuine emotion. I suppose unconsciously I'd not wanted to believe it. She had so much else that was enviable, I'd preferred to regard her as lacking the capacity for deep human feeling. Now, viewing her objectively, I knew that the curve of her lower lip alone gave the lie to such prejudiced nonsense. Warmth, in the maternal sense, she might lack, but not the capacity for passion. Passion checkreined, disciplined by her will, no doubt; yet nonetheless a force in her nature. And one untouched by David, I'd have sworn. . . . He could, though, build her a castle.

Build me a castle
Forty feet high,
So I can see her
As she rides by.

As she rides by, love,
As she rides by . . .

When the final haunting note had died away, Kevin said, albeit with reluctance, "I'm afraid it's your bedtime, Johnny."

Before the child could protest, Rosamond had risen, taken charge. "It's late," she said, "for everyone."

And although she took care to stay outside the radius of the lamps after Brad had turned them on, she gave no outward sign of turmoil.

I told myself I might have read too much into her one unguarded moment. Unaccountably, it was for David's sake I hoped I had.

7

There were no more concerts.

Plainly Rosamond had vetoed them. Brad did not say so outright, but he had no need to say so; it was she who arranged each day's program.

Whether I was right in my belief that her reason was a determination not to be stirred emotionally, the result was a return to the more humdrum pattern of earlier evenings.

After dinner everyone so inclined played some game or other, chiefly as a means of not falling asleep before the early bedtime hour. Or rather, speaking for myself, on whom the mountain air and increasingly long hours of riding in the August sun had a powerfully soporific effect, this was the main purpose to be served. It was far from being everyone's.

David would gladly have sat all night at the bridge table. He was one of the people whom the altitude overstimulated; incomparably more important, this was his sole opportunity of being with Rosamond for any appreciable length of time away from the watchful eyes of his daughter.

The mere setup of the ranch was an obstacle to privacy; and although I had no doubt that Rosamond's ingenuity could have overcome this obstacle, neither did I doubt the soundness of her judgment in failing to do so. It would have been worse than unwise to add fuel to the flames of Dorothy's jealousy; it would have been wanton folly.

For Dorothy was the key figure in the situation, as I learned from no less an authority than her father, the day after their arrival.

It was that in-between hour of five in the afternoon; I was sitting on the porch of our cabin, nodding over a volume of Gesell, when David came to call.

"If I'm not interrupting you?"

I laughed, putting the book on the table beside my chair. "I haven't turned a page for at least ten minutes. I can't read anything out here—which is one of the blessings of the place."

David seated himself on the step, his back resting against the log that supported the roof of the porch. He had already acquired the beginning of a sun tan, as well as a serviceable blue denim work shirt. My initial liking for him grew apace as he spoke of Jim; there was insight and discrimination in his praise. He asked presently about the children; to my surprise he even knew their names, knew that Josiah was six months old and Lucinda two and a half years.

As parent to parent he then mentioned his own daughter.

We could not see the swimming pool from here but we could occasionally hear the shrieks of one of the intrepid souls plunging into the icy water fed by mountain streams. Dorothy was of this number, as was Jim. Kevin and Johnny were down there too.

"Dorothy's a fine swimmer," David said. "And she sat her horse better this morning than her old father did his. Once she makes up her mind to do something, she goes through with it."

This I suspected was true; I'd already seen evidence of both her stamina and her stubbornness.

"I think it's going to do her a world of good to be out here with all you young people," David went on. "She didn't want to come; she made one excuse after another. That's why I had to put off coming until so late."

"You couldn't have come without her?"

He seemed startled by the question. "There would have been no point to it," he said.

Then he told me the whole story.

It began with Dorothy's mother, for whom she had been named. Even after all these years there was wonder and gratitude, and pain, in David's voice when he mentioned that other Dorothy. She had married him when he had nothing to offer, and in face of the violent opposition of her mother, who as a widow controlled the plant in which he then worked for a modest weekly wage.

David looked away from me, his long-fingered slender hand pulling up by the roots the tall blades of grass near the step, as he spoke of his wife's death, for which plainly he had been made to feel responsible.

Expecting a second child, she had nevertheless, unknown to him, attempted to paint the walls of an improvised nursery and fallen from a high step ladder. The child had been born prematurely and had not lived; she herself had survived a matter only of hours. But during those last hours she had asked David, by all they held sacred, to look after Dorothy always.

A considerable moment elapsed before David was able to resume.

"Dorothy was only three years old; her grandmother carried her off to the big house on the hill that very day. She insisted on keeping her there. I wasn't thinking very straight about anything just then. I couldn't afford to hire anyone competent to bring Dorothy up; I wasn't going to be separated from her. So when my mother-in-law suggested I live there, too, I gave in. I see now it was a terrible mistake."

"I don't see what else you could have done."

"There didn't seem to be any alternative at the time," he admitted. "And of course I regarded the arrangement as only temporary; to tide us over until I'd made enough money for a separate establishment, suitable for a little girl. Dorothy and I used to talk a great deal about the house we were going to build some day, and the fun we were going to have in it. It was one of our favorite games. As she got older, she began to plan the parties we'd give, where she'd act as hostess."

I was the one who now avoided David's eyes. Clearly he had no conception of the brutal impact of the blow his projected second marriage must have dealt Dorothy. It was immeasurably worse than the natural resentment mingled with shame that any grown daughter might feel at seeing her father in the throes of enchantment. What David inadvertently had done was to shatter the dream he himself had fostered in Dorothy's mind.

With only half an ear I had been aware of his going on, "But I did what all too many men do, I suppose. I started out with the intention of making money so that I could give Dorothy everything I didn't have when I was young; and then before I knew it, I'd become so absorbed in the plant itself, I regarded it as an end, not a means. And so I let life slip by."

Until you met Rosamond, I mentally supplied.

Sounds from the swimming pool indicated the group was breaking up. "Who wants a Coke?" Johnny was calling.

David got to his feet. He said quietly in conclusion, "Before I could persuade Dorothy to come out here, I told her the promise I'd given her mother still held good. That I'd not make any irrevocable decision that she opposed, once she knew at first-hand what the factors involved were and had given it sober thought. There's not as much time left as I'd like; but that can't be helped now. As a practical matter, I'll have to give an answer before September first about selling the plant. Which only leaves three weeks."

He shook his head, trying to smile. "Although whether I could stand the strain longer than that, I'm none too sure."

It seemed infamous that any nineteen-year-old girl should possess such power, hold the fate of five other people in her hands. Yet in view of her father's character I could see that it was not superstition but simple self-knowledge that told him he would never enjoy a moment's peace of mind if he tried to seize his own happiness at the cost of his only child's.

Whether he would have felt this way had only the question of marriage been involved, was academic; there would be no marriage unless he quit both the plant and Ohio. Nor would David have wanted it otherwise. It would be a new and enchanted world into which Rosamond would lead him.

A world that also had a vast amount to offer Dorothy that she sorely needed.

The crucial problem, however, was whether Dorothy could be brought to recognize that need. And whatever other gaps there might have been in David's perception, he'd been made aware of her instant hostility to Rosamond.

Therefore, to repeat, his periods of greatest contentment became those evening hours spent out of the range of his daughter's vision.

The bridge table was always set up in the living room; freeing the cardroom for the noisier games of twenty-one or penny ante in which I joined by choice, leaving Jim and Brad to their running bridge tournament with David and Rosamond.

Even in the cardroom there were usually two separate groups, save on rare occasions when Mary joined us. Dorothy and Johnny occasionally played Scrabble until his bedtime, when she would leave with him; more often she took him for a ride in the big convertible to Moose in quest of ice-cream cones. She seemed to have a chip on her shoulder so far as everyone else was concerned, with the exception of Johnny's uncle Kevin.

This was not, however, an environment in which the carrot-topped young doctor shone. Kevin was no horseman, nor in the least handsome; when the burn vanished from his face it was replaced by freckles. His manner was no less unromantic; he treated Dorothy as he might have treated a teen-age sister of whom he was fond.

Between Susan and Dorothy, the antagonism of the first day had settled into a state of armed truce. Dorothy relegated me to the enemy's camp, because Susan treated me as friend. Amos was under the same banner, although not for the same ostensible reason. His discovery that on her own home grounds Susan could not only outride him, but possessed skills and knowledge of animal lore not included in his curriculum at Cambridge, led to increased efforts on his part to show up the gaps in her scholastic knowledge.

A puerile form of manifesting attraction, from my view, and one Susan did not recognize as such either. Yet Jim stoutly maintained this was its source, whenever the subject was mentioned.

This was about the only matter connected with the ranch we ever did discuss, during that period of feverish uncertainty, although we refrained from choice, not from lack of opportunity. After Spike's advent we always rode alone, our various friends at other ranches providing both a welcome change from the slopes of Vesuvius atmosphere, as well as a legitimate excuse for our independent excursions.

Sunday had been the sole exception. Being Spike's day off, we'd ridden with the others to the picnic grounds some three miles up the Snake, where Mary and Brad joined us in the station wagon. On the theory of saving Mary trouble, Brad, as titular chef, presided over an elaborate charcoal grille; while Mary, as assistant, probably did no more than twice as much work than if we'd lunched comfortably at home.

It was not fondness for the picnic grounds as such, but the sudden recollection that it was there, as timekeeper, I'd last used my missing wristwatch that caused us to make a detour on our way home from the next Friday's lengthy expedition.

Approaching the plateau from the much higher land of this unfamiliar route, we found ourselves confronted by an unexpected problem. We'd started out early this morning; and now must either ride an extra mile in the broiling midafternoon sun to reach the path where the ascent was gradual, or risk descending a virtually straight up and down trail, rocky to boot, that would have tested the sure-footedness of a mountain goat.

We reined our horses to talk it over. Jim thought the trail was much too steep for me, an opinion in which I was about to concur when he surprised me by saying, in an oddly embarrassed tone, "Maybe we'd better let the watch go for today. I promised David I'd be back not later than four thirty."

"Don't tell me you're going to play bridge before dinner?"

"Certainly not. No, this is a professional appointment."

Jim's self-consciousness in itself revealed the importance he attached to the appointment; moreover, he'd been in a state of suppressed excitement throughout the day. Ever since David had drawn him aside after breakfast for a private word, I now recalled. David had looked dazed.

Only one conclusion was possible. Yet it went contrary to everything I'd come to believe.

8

"David's going to buy the ranch!" I said explicitly.

At Jim's nod the sky became a lovelier blue, the sun's rays beneficent warmth rather than oppressive heat. Until this very moment I'd not dared admit the full extent of my foreboding, the fear inseparable from the conviction, that the project was doomed to failure.

This would mean everything to Mary.

And to Brad and Susan too.

I laughed out loud, realizing I'd forgotten what it would mean to David.

"Does Rosamond know about it?" I asked.

Jim's laughter rang out. "Yes," he said, when he could speak, "that trifling detail was attended to before I was called in. David even has the strange idea that Rosamond's consenting to marry him is what counts most."

"You didn't tell me that."

"But without it, there would be no ranch deal. No sale of the plant. Nothing."

Just as pleased as I was, Jim confessed he'd had a tough time in keeping still all day. It had not been a matter of legal ethics but of unwillingness to deprive David of the chance to make the announcement himself, which he planned to do tomorrow evening. Tomorrow was his birthday; some time ago he'd invited all of us to go into Jackson for a spree.

"But since you know the gist of the matter, you might as well know the details," Jim said. "You may remember that the bridge game broke up early last night. Well, the reason was that Dorothy came into the living room around ten o'clock and asked her father if she could see him for a moment when he was dummy. They went out to the kitchen together. David wasn't gone long but when he came back, alone, he was walking on air.

"He told me this morning what had happened. Dorothy said she'd already had enough time to think things over. And she wanted him to know, as a sort of advance birthday present, that she didn't want to stand in the way of his happiness. The general idea was, 'You've got your own life to lead and I've got mine'; . . . I certainly have misjudged that girl," Jim added.

I had misjudged her shamefully, believing her antagonism to Rosamond had deepened with each passing day and not crediting her with enough generosity of spirit to ignore her own feelings. I had also wondered whether Rosamond herself, put to the test, her conditions fulfilled, would consent to marry David.

On both counts I'd been proved wrong. And never had I been more pleased by being wrong.

With my eye I again measured the precipitous rocky trail between us and the picnic grounds. It was still far too steep for me.

"Let's forget about my watch and go straight home," I glanced up to say. "We'll be back here Sunday anyway."

Jim was not listening. He was gazing into the distance with the Indian scout look which usually means he's sighted moose or deer. There were apt to be both on the islands of the Snake.

This time, however, he'd sighted the cavalcade from our ranch, also on their way home; I could not understand his scowl.

To be sure they had not yet made the requisite cutoff from the road that led along the treacherous shore; but both Susan and Rosamond were of the party, and even young Johnny knew the hazards of that intervening no man's land where the underpinnings of the bank had been swept away in the spring floods.

They were all strung out in a long line, without crowding; their pace was leisurely. Each one followed the example of Susan, in the lead, turning his horse off the road into the sage well before he reached the dangerous point of land jutting out over the swirling water of the river.

Spike Noland, on his beautiful black horse, was bringing up the rear. As he approached the cutoff, instead of turning he let out a sudden war whoop.

"Yipee!" he yelled, so loud it re-echoed even up here.

Raising one arm commandingly, he spurred Diamond into a gallop, raced full tilt toward the death trap.

Diamond had more sense than his master; he stopped so abruptly Spike was jolted up out of the saddle a perceptible foot or more.

He wheeled the horse around, returned to the starting post. This time he made more careful preparation. His upraised hand was not empty now. Raking Diamond's flanks with his spurs, he made a second try. Nearing the spot where the trick horse had balked before, a pistol shot shattered the air. Diamond leaped forward. The ground gave way. Horse and rider vanished.

Without conscious volition I found myself descending the rocky trail before me, miraculously still in the saddle at its bottom, though my feet were out of the stirrups.

Rosamond had instantly assumed command. "Susan! Amos! Keep everyone back! I'll go down!"

Off she started, full speed, on the buckskin toward the path leading down to the river a quarter of a mile farther on. A path no less skilled a rider could have negotiated.

She'd picked her deputies wisely; Jim appointed himself a third. All the horses had been frightened by the pistol shot; the steadiest and most dependable, the gentle mare assigned to Johnny, who usually had difficulty in urging her into a fast trot, had now been the first to go berserk. Rearing and plunging like a thing possessed, then breaking into the frenzied run worse than the roughest of gallops.

I saw the child's terror-stricken face as they flashed by. With difficulty getting the toes of my boots into the stirrups, I was almost thrown over my horse's head as he started in pursuit. I thought my arms would be pulled from the sockets in effort to hold him back.

Nor would I have succeeded if Susan and Jim and Amos had not formed a cordon, so to speak. Amos, cutting across the sagebrush without benefit of path, was able to outdistance Johnny's mare, reach the head of the procession. He turned up a long, relatively steep, incline at a brisk but not breakneck speed.

Horses being in some instances like sheep, God be thanked, Johnny's followed the leader, and mine followed his.

Now that the danger was over I felt shaken, sick with retrospective fear. Johnny might have been killed. I myself might have been. I thought of the children.

Glancing down from the plateau toward the river, I caught sight of a black hat rising above the bluff. A second later Rosamond materialized, safely in the saddle. Once her horse was on solid ground she sped in the direction of the ranch so swiftly as to be lost from view long before the rest of us were halfway there.

The way back by this roundabout route seemed endless. Numbly I rejoiced at seeing that the ranch gate had been opened.

I blinked, scarcely able to believe my eyes.

The gate had been opened by none other than Spike Noland, his shirt plastered to his back, dark hair wet, seated on his dripping-wet black horse, showing his fine white teeth as he laughed.

And far from being glad that he was alive, uninjured, I hated him as I have never hated anyone.

It was sheer rage that lent me the strength to dismount. The earth seemed to move beneath my feet. What Jim might do, I dared not contemplate. He listened in silence to Spike's braggadocio account of how easy it had been, rolling with Diamond over the cliff, then swimming a little piece downstream before climbing back up to the road. In silence Jim unsaddled our horses, turned them loose. He lighted a cigarette, his hand a shade unsteady, although less so than my knees.

He said nothing until we were well away from the corral, walking slowly up the road. Susan was out of earshot, having hurried ahead to join Rosamond, who'd ridden the buckskin to the hitching rail near the garage, and was now dismounting. It was Dorothy's comment that set Jim off.

"Spike might have been drowned!" she said with admiration tinged by awe.

"I'm glad he wasn't," Jim said quietly. "Drowning would be far too good for him."

"Truer words were never spoken," Kevin said. His face seemed white beneath its freckles. He put one hand on his nephew's head as if tangibly to assure himself the boy was alive, unharmed.

Johnny wriggled loose. Now that the danger was over, he'd forgotten his mortal terror. Which was natural, perhaps, in a child of ten. It was also natural that this forgetfulness, manifesting itself in a defiant "Spike was brave!" should have aroused Kevin's fury.

For the first time I heard an acrimonious interchange between them.

"You ought to be old enough to understand the cruelty, the criminal stupidity, of that stunt of his!"

"Nobody was hurt, were they? You're stupid yourself to say it was cruel. You're just jealous, that's all."

"Of Spike's horse?" Kevin said ironically. "It was only Diamond I cared about."

"My sentiment exactly," Amos said.

He had been fighting to control himself, I realized, having seen his hands clenching and unclenching, I remembered too that Jim had told me in confidence about the psychic scars left by the bodily wounds Amos had received in Korea: a revulsion against physical violence amounting to a phobia.

Dorothy wheeled around. She had walked quickly ahead after Jim's blast; now she blocked our way.

I had the eerie sense of being confronted by a stranger. Nearly two weeks in this sun and wind had brought warm rose and tan to her cheeks, pleasing golden lights to her sandy hair. Her initial shyness had vanished with her pallor. Indeed the stance of her tall slender figure in jodhpurs and striped shirt was self-assured to the point of arrogance.

"I've never seen anything so thrilling in all my life!" she declared, as if that settled it, no more need be said.

"Haven't you?" Kevin asked with razor-sharp irony. Not for nothing was his hair bright red. "You should have seen the psychopath I saw just before I left New York. He climbed out on the ledge of a hotel room twenty stories high above the street and stayed there for hours and hours, thrilling the crowds below, sending women into hysterics, almost causing the death of the policemen who finally saved him. And put him behind bars."

If Dorothy had been infuriated, as Johnny was, by Kevin's effort to debunk Spike, her attitude could have been put into the same pigeonhole of childish hero worship.

Not that I wouldn't still have itched to smack her. But Dorothy showed no sign of anger. Instead she smiled; the superior, pitying smile of one who's reached a lofty summit unscalable by ordinary mortals.

As flagrant a danger sign as a printed placard: "Man At Work."

But when did she ever have a chance to see Spike, other than in a group?

I was too shaken to think straight, and it was not until evening came that the answer was sickeningly clear.

Dorothy and Johnny again departed from the cardroom, headed for the convertible, allegedly bound for the soda fountain in Moose. There was a soda fountain there, true; but Moose was also the place where Spike kept his trailer.

9

Kevin's unnatural quiet after Dorothy and his nephew had disappeared from the cardroom led me to suspect his thoughts might have followed the same disturbing course as mine. In a sense, I hoped that this was true. For if Dorothy were using these trips to Moose with Johnny as a pretext for clandestine meetings with Spike, Kevin was the one person on the ranch who might be able to deal wisely and competently with the situation. He possessed insight and compassion far beyond his twenty-six years.

Then as I glanced from his engagingly homely face to his red hair, I remembered that he also possessed a hot temper, admirably though he kept it under control. He had, however, clashed with Dorothy this afternoon. Which left her without a single friend her own age. With only a ten-year-old child as companion. This was her own fault, I told myself. Although without conviction, when I thought of her background, conditioning. The domineering grandmother who had treated Dorothy, even when grown, as if she were an infant. The long-cherished dream of escape Dorothy had harbored, of a future bound up with her father. A dream smashed to bits by his meeting Rosamond and falling head over heels in love.

Yes, it was easy to find justification for Dorothy. When she was not present in person. The trouble was, the more charitable my attitude, the deeper became my anxiety.

That this mood was not conducive to strict attention to the game of twenty-one in which ostensibly I was engaging, together with Kevin and Susan and Amos, was brought home to me by Susan, after an interminable hour of sitting at the card table.

"Elizabeth, it's a shame to take your money," she said, again collecting my pennies. "Wouldn't you like to call it a day?"

I lost no time in rising, then perforce delayed a moment longer to discuss tomorrow's plans. Mary and I were going into town early in the morning on a shopping expedition, partly with David's birthday in mind. In the evening he was giving a gala dinner in town.

Susan's head was in the clouds; enthralled by the dazzling future Rosamond's marriage to David would ensure, she spoke with gay extravagance of the night club in Jackson.

Amos listened with disdain, real or assumed. He said sardonically when she paused, "Wait until you get to the Stork Club in New York. I'm sure you'll have a *succès fou;* bowl them over with your description of the wonderful dams the busy little beavers make out here."

"Probably I will," Susan said, her tone demure, her eyes bright as stars. "New Yorkers always seem eager to learn about new and interesting things."

"We thank you," Kevin said, making a little bow to her and then to me.

But after he'd helped me on with my coat and we had started outside, the smile left his face.

The instant we were beyond earshot, while his hand was still on the door he'd closed behind us, he said, "I wish to high heaven I'd not blown my top this afternoon! Antagonized Dorothy—"

He stopped quite still, at the sound of a muffled sob.

A heartbreaking, terrifying sob.

In one long stride he reached the chair on the porch where Johnny was huddled.

The child's eyes seemed enormous; struggling manfully against tears, it was a full and awful moment before he was able to answer Kevin's quiet, "What's the matter, Johnny?"

"I was j-just waiting for you." His teeth were chattering.

"You could have come in and got me," Kevin said with an assumption of lightness that seemed nothing short of magnificent. "But I guess you had a cramp or pain of some sort that made you want to sit down. Maybe the sort of pain you had last year before your appendix came out?"

"No," Johnny said and got to his feet. He was shivering; he swallowed hard before he was able to say, beseechingly, "You're going to bed now, aren't you, Uncle Kevin?"

"I thought I'd go down to our cabin, yes. But I'm not sleepy. I've got all the time in the world to find out what's wrong, if you don't feel well."

"I feel all right. Honest I do."

And now that he was assured Kevin would go with him to the cabin, Johnny had stopped trembling. Plainly he'd been frightened, scared out of his wits.

I could have wept when he put his hand in mine as we started across the lawn in the moonlight. "It's kind of hard to see the path," he said with pretended nonchalance, as if I were the one in need of aid.

His hand was cold to the touch, and there was a world of homesickness for his mother in the tightness with which it clung to my hand. He seemed so reluctant to have me leave when we reached the first of our two neighboring cabins, I said I'd find a magazine for him to read and take it over later.

Purposely I delayed until Kevin had been able to make a thorough examination. By the time I went in, Johnny was in bed, his eyes almost closed in sleep. He yawned widely, telling me good night.

"There's nothing wrong physically that I can find," Kevin followed me outside to say. "And I know Johnny well enough to know from the way he answered my questions that Dorothy isn't to blame. At least not directly. . . . It may be a case of deferred shock. The aftermath of the runaway this afternoon."

By morning Kevin had discarded this theory. He and Johnny arrived together in the dining room just as I was leaving; of the two, Kevin showed greater sign of stress and strain. It was not until some time later, when I was starting in the general direction of the garage, that I saw Kevin alone.

Johnny had wakened several times during the night, he said; each time to make sure his uncle was there. But the only words he'd uttered that might throw light on this sudden abnormal timidity, was the question he'd worked around to asking with elaborate circumlocution. He'd begun by talking about firearms in general, then gone on to say, "Could a tiny little pistol, just a few inches long, kill anyone?"

Spike owned such a pistol in addition to the larger one he'd fired yesterday, Kevin knew. "He must have threatened Johnny with it." As further evidence, when the plans for the day had been discussed at breakfast, Johnny had declared he wouldn't go riding. Then he'd learned that Spike had been assigned chores that would keep him at the ranch. "Johnny's now hell-bent on riding. And he's overjoyed by the prospect of going home with Mrs. Pritchett this afternoon to spend the night. He's in there now, packing his suitcase."

Mrs. Pritchett herself, resplendent in lavender dimity, was coming in our direction. "I've made up the cabin," I told her.

"Well, that's mighty nice of you," she said. Shattering all precedent, she'd agreed to cook lunch. "Dorothy made hers up too, she just told me. She's going to town with you."

Damn! I thought, having looked forward to the trip with Mary, who had almost no leisure these days.

Glancing over Mrs. Pritchett's Junoesque shoulder, I saw Dorothy standing beside the station wagon, wearing the same beige dress and large blue sunglasses she'd worn on her arrival.

Most of the men were standing on the lawn by the sundial, the favorite congregating place at this time of day. David came forward to intercept me.

Would I go to the Wort Hotel and order the finest dinner for tonight they could produce for ten people? And champagne, if they had first-rate champagne.

They had the best of everything, I assured him.

"Good. Use your own judgment about the menu." He laughed. "And include nails if you want to. I can eat anything again. No more yellow pills— Why, what's this?"

A cloud of dust beyond the curve of the road heralded the emergence of two swiftly approaching riders; Susan and Rosamond were racing toward us, both riding bareback, both expert enough to slow their horses into a canter, then a fast walk, and bring them almost to a halt near the hitching rail. Whereupon in unison they slid off onto the ground.

It was, as David said, as pretty a performance as one could wish to see. "And as pretty a pair of performers," he added as they advanced toward us on foot.

With this also I agreed. Rosamond was in high spirits, exuberant in a way I'd not hitherto seen, and that made ridiculous my secret conviction that she was marrying David solely at the cool dictates of her head. There were dancing lights in her blue eyes as she smiled up at him beneath the straight-brimmed black hat.

She turned then to Brad. "It's so heavenly a day, I think Taggart would be just right, don't you? David hasn't been there yet and the color of the lake will be breath-taking."

"It sounds fine," Brad said, as he probably would have said if she'd suggested a trip to Mars.

And if she'd made up her mind to organize such a trip, it probably would be successful, I thought after she too had drawn me aside to ask if I'd do her a favor.

Would I buy on approval a present for David, in case the one she'd ordered from New York failed to arrive by the noon mail today?

"I'm hoping against hope it will," she said. "I'm going to check. But I don't dare count on it. And you can imagine how horrid it would be, to be empty-handed."

She seemed so human in her concern I came close to succumbing utterly to her charm. Without dint of heroic effort I was able to keep my record unblemished, however, for she went on to give me specific, detailed instructions providing for every conceivable contingency. She was a perfectionist, I granted; but I had a hairdressing appointment as well as a mile-long shopping list.

Meanwhile Mary had appeared; attired as usual in blue jeans and a boy's white shirt, the only sign of the day's difference, the large woven bag slung over one arm. No, there was another difference: she looked bemused. Her incredulity was not the incredulity of joy stamped in David's slender suntanned face, but the superstitious fear of one to whom good fortune has long been a stranger.

I felt certain, seeing her rap on the wooden frame of her shopping bag as David and Brad began discussing favorable sites for the building of additional cabins, that she would not be able to believe the end of the rainbow had in fact been reached until the actual deeds of the ranch had been signed, sealed and recorded with the county clerk. Which they would be on Monday. Until then, although there were only forty-eight hours to go, Mary would keep right on fearing that once again there would be some last-minute hitch, some unforeseeable accident.

She turned, startled, as Dorothy called out, "Aren't we ever going to leave?"

"Well, for goodness sake, I didn't notice you over there," Mary said. "We're going in your car, anyway. Brad's got to use the station wagon; he's going up to Moran."

"Why not the Littles' coupé?" Dorothy said.

"Because it won't be large enough to hold all the things I have to buy."

David stared at his daughter in astonishment. Whatever reproof he might have uttered remained unsaid. Silently he waited until she'd reluctantly got in behind the wheel of the powerful convertible and backed it out of the garage into the driveway, then he opened the door so Mary and I could get in.

"Drive carefully," he said.

And whether because he said it or because Dorothy was churned up inside, she drove far too fast for safety; accelerating as she neared the bunkhouse, recklessly swinging the long car around the sharp curve.

"Stop that!" Mary said. "Maybe your life isn't worth anything to you, but Elizabeth and I feel different about ours. If you don't want to drive, say so, and one of us will be glad to."

Dorothy's face seemed to crumple. "I'm sorry," she said; and drove the rest of the way with care although without speaking until we were within the city limits and Mary asked a direct question. "Can you do all you've got to do by twelve thirty?"

"Gracious, yes," Dorothy kept her gaze straight ahead. "All I've got to do is to buy a present for Dad. And cash a check first."

The bank was also my first stop. We walked there together, leaving Mary and the convertible at the market nearby. I'd filled out my check in advance, and having been identified on an earlier occasion, had no difficulty in cashing it. I had turned away from the window to stow the bills in my wallet when the cashier called me back. Dorothy had now presented her check. "Would you mind endorsing this, Mrs. Little? . . . A mere formality," he added courteously.

I could only hope so, as he slid the check face upward toward me. Dorothy must be closing out her account in the Ohio bank on which it was drawn, judging from the odd amount: $2823.19. It also seemed to me a huge amount. I had no doubt about her possessing it, however; I picked up the pen and signed.

"You must be going to buy a quarter horse for your father," I said when we were out on the wooden sidewalk.

"That's right," she said quickly. Far too quickly to be convincing.

But what she did intend to buy in the town of Jackson with the better part of three thousand dollars was of no slightest concern to me. Until some thirty minutes after we'd parted in front of Miss McClung's Beauty Salon.

10

The strong dexterous fingers of Miss McClung, massaging needed oil into my scalp, drove all thought from my mind. By the time the shampoo was finished, I had reached a state of euphoria. That it was of brief duration was no fault of Miss McClung's.

Pearl among women, she made no protest at my setting the wave myself and disappeared until I was ready for the dryer. Returning then, she handed me a new movie magazine. "Your friend over there sent it."

It was a second before I recognized the friend, whose hair was now pinned flat to her head, as the pretty wife of a classmate of Jim's at whose ranch we'd lunched a couple of days ago. With an impish grin she pointed to the magazine.

A folder of matches marked the salient pages. In the margin an arrow drawn with lipstick directed attention to the caption beneath the photograph of a dazzling blonde in elaborate rodeo costume mounted on a beautiful black horse:

"'Lariat Lothario good riddance, trick horse mourned,' says Starlet Bianca Maldeen."

A paragraph later, the unmourned ex-husband was cursorily identified as "One Spike Noland, former small bit stunt rider."

The factual content of the piece boiled down to this: Bianca Maldeen, in Reno to divorce a previous husband, had met Spike Noland, in due course married him, then exerted her influence to obtain parts for him in Western pictures. A kindness he'd repaid by all manner of indignities, the crowning outrage having been his decamping with the fabulously valuable and cherished steed, Black Diamond, she'd generously permitted him to ride in one picture.

She had won an uncontested divorce from him, in California.

The decree would not become final for another four months, I was inordinately relieved to find, and read on.

The interviewer gave it as her personal opinion—which in Hollywood fashion meant she laid it down as the law of the Medes and Persians—that even if he had not been boycotted by all the studios, Spike Noland would never again dare cross the state line into California.

Which might explain his returning here to Jackson Hole, taking a job as wrangler.

In memory I saw the check Dorothy had cashed. And a terrifying possibility occurred to me. Suppose Spike had persuaded her to buy Diamond as a birthday present for her father? Unknown to her, he might have frightened Johnny in order to prevent his overhearing these negotiations. Suppose further, David attempted to ride the spirited animal. It would be child's play then for someone of Spike's experience to pull the strings so that without any blame ever attaching to himself, David would be fatally injured. Leaving Dorothy, as affairs now stood, in sole and undisputed possession of a vast fortune.

Well, that was a plan that could easily be forestalled; the hypothetical chain of events broken at its vital link. David had utmost faith in Jim's judgment; Jim would be able to persuade him not to get within ten feet of

Diamond. So there was no cause for alarm even if my most morbid suspicions were warranted.

And they probably weren't, I told myself for about the fiftieth time when I neared the market, at twelve twenty-five, arms piled high with packages, one of which included a copy of the movie magazine I'd bought at the hotel newsstand for Jim's delectation.

Dorothy and Mary were standing on the sidewalk in front of the convertible. As I drew near I found a crisis had developed.

Piled up on the curb were half a dozen cases of canned and bottled goods, together with wooden crates containing fruits and vegetables and meat, together with staples. Two clerks were waiting to load them into the luggage compartment.

Dorothy refused to unlock it. "There's no room there," she declared, her cheeks flaming. "It's full of old coats and stuff."

"We can take them out and put them on the back seat until we get home," Mary said reasonably, although the flash of fire in her blue eyes showed with what difficulty she was controlling her temper. "Otherwise, I won't be able to take all this stuff."

Dorothy's lips closed in a tight stubborn line. She got in behind the wheel, keeping both hands over her tan leather purse as if fearful the keys would be snatched from her.

One of the clerks said jocosely, "Guess there must be a dead body in there with those old coats."

The fury in Dorothy's glance seemed proof that he'd hit the mark; that she'd hidden something she did not want anyone to see.

A saddle for her father? But there would be no need to conceal that; not unless she'd bought Spike's silver-mounted saddle for some exorbitant price. Even then, we'd see it sooner or later.

Mary's voice was husky with suppressed rage as she conceded defeat, directing the young men to take back into the store everything but the perishables.

"Your hair looks nice, Elizabeth," she said as she motioned me to get into the front seat; she herself got into the back, crowded though it was by parcels. She said nothing more until we were approaching the half-dozen log buildings that comprised the way station of Moose. "I'll have to stop here for ice cream. Johnny never seems to have enough."

She had spoken in good faith; indirection was not in her character. Dorothy winced, however; involuntarily glancing toward Spike's trailer.

I got out when Mary did, although my purpose was to get the mail. And what a lot of time I'd wasted in town, I thought, as the postmistress handed me, in addition to the stack of letters and Brad's New York newspaper, a box sent by air express from an impressive Fifth Avenue haberdashery, addressed to Mrs. Rosamond Conner.

As I started toward the car, an unfamiliar voice asked if I'd kindly wait a moment. "That's a cowgirl I want to snap."

Following the direction in which his camera was pointed, I saw Rosamond, mounted on her buckskin horse, waiting on the other side of the well-traveled thoroughfare for a chance to cross. An enchanting picture she made, too; even before I held up the box so she would see it. Then with a dazzling smile and a wave of her gloved hand, she turned the horse's head and galloped homeward.

She must have flown diagonally across the fields. By the time we reached the garage, the buckskin was tied to the hitching rail; Rosamond was waiting by the kitchen entrance when we stopped there to unload.

With the elation of a schoolgirl, although a well-mannered schoolgirl, she thanked me for buying the now unnecessary cuff links; which she said, superfluously, she'd return herself, and streaked off toward her cabin, both arms clutched around the precious box.

"My lands, is that what all the excitement was about?" Mrs. Pritchett said, stowing the ice cream in the freezing compartment of the refrigerator, pending the return from Taggart of the rest of the company. "I'd expected something about the size of an elephant, from the way she was steamed up; I'll bet those long-distance wires were sizzling. Still and all," she added, "from the way Mr. Ferensen's face fell when he found she couldn't go along on the ride this morning, I guess he'd treasure a cotton bandanna handkerchief, if she gave it to him."

"Any cotton bandanna that store sold would be labeled 'handwoven in Italy' and cost a good twenty dollars," I said abstractedly, starting outside again, mindful that I must dispose of the rest of the mail before I did anything else.

A picture postcard brought a smile to my lips, a reflection of the smiling family group of three, photographed on a street corner in Paris. It was not the parents who caught my eye, young and attractive though they were, but the beguiling roly-poly little girl, five or six years old, with two pigtails of ribbon-tied hair over her shoulders.

I turned the card over, simultaneously saw the message: "Will be with you almost as soon as you get this" and the address: "Master John Humphreys."

The family group must represent Johnny's mother, his as yet unknown and bitterly resented stepfather, and his new stepsister. The affectionate manner in which she was holding his mother's arm now seemed unfortunate. Johnny might believe he'd been relegated to second place; and it could be an agonizing emotion for a child.

Or for a grownup, I was to emend, although not with commiseration, before many hours had passed.

11

"This must seem like awfully small potatoes to you, compared to New York," Brad said stiffly, seating himself beside me at the table overlooking the dance floor where David had suggested we adjourn for coffee and liqueurs.

We had just finished a superb dinner built around the tenderest of Kansas steaks and driest of French champagnes. The music was so lively I fairly ached to be dancing. I had brought with me a sense of supreme well-being unattainable in any city.

"For my money," I said, "this has New York beat a mile."

"That's very polite of you."

"No; the merest statement of fact."

Of all senseless arguments, I thought impatiently. Presumably Brad was remembering with nostalgia the New York he'd last known as a Princeton under-graduate twenty-odd years ago. But his nostalgia was no longer excusable. His long exile was practically ended; he would be going East again this winter, with the legitimate excuse of interviewing prospective dudes for the enlarged ranch of next summer. Susan would be there, enjoying what he called the advantages, under Rosamond's expert tutelage, backed by David's impressive fortune.

Brad ought to be on the crest of the wave; instead he was devoid even of the geniality that hitherto had seemed as indigenous to his nature as his ruddy dark complexion and heavy-set build.

"Now that the old Ritz has been torn down," I said, forced by his silence and the vacant chair on my other side to say something, and deciding to make it emphatic, "this is my favorite hotel anywhere. And even at the Ritz, you'd never have seen such a picturesque cross section of humanity."

I glanced beyond him out into the Silver Dollar bar, where the customers were standing three-deep its full curved length. The most exaggeratedly Western in attire might well be tourists, but this in no way marred the colorful effect.

Brad's answer was a shrug; a markedly ungracious gesture from someone of his usual courtesy. He had been unlike himself ever since he'd hurried in late for luncheon, I recalled. His trip to Moran had occupied the better part of the morning; I'd assumed the unwonted exertion had tired him. His heart condition might be more serious than I'd somehow believed.

The orchestra struck up "La Varsovienne." I saw Jim rise; in answer to my silently willing him to, I thought. Then I saw that it was Rosamond he was asking to dance to our favorite tune. As of course simple good manners demanded that he should, I told myself. Just as if she and David were already married, Rosamond had acted as hostess at dinner.

She knew the right steps, I admitted, noting the expert movements of her slim feet in wisps of high-heeled red sandals, the graceful swirling of her full-skirted rose and red print dress. There was a Latin quality in her appearance tonight, due in part to the beautiful earrings of antique paste hanging almost to her shoulders.

I turned to Brad, about to say, "Rosamond looks like one of the Spanish countesses in the fashion magazines." The words died on my lips.

He too was gazing at his cousin. But there was a somberness in his dark eyes, a look of desolation that robbed me of speech. If he'd lost his last friend in the world he could not have seemed more forlorn, bereft.

I found it hard indeed to take. My tolerance for jealousy had been exhausted before the end of luncheon.

Young Johnny had used a burnt match to draw a moustache on the face of the beguiling small girl photographed with his mother, then had taken out his pocket knife and begun to cut off her braids. "If that stupid little jerk ever dares come out here, I'll scalp her, see?"

Johnny was only ten, though; Brad was thirty years older. His silence at midday now connected itself in my mind with Rosamond's handsome gift to David, well meriting her tizzy: half a dozen shirts of finest flannel, each of a different delectable color. David was proudly wearing the soft green one tonight.

I'd felt a pang of sympathy for Dorothy's stricken look. Her present for her father had proved to be two locally purchased flamboyant plaid shirts. She had pretended brittle unconcern. The same brittleness, transmuted into a slightly feverish gaiety, had tided her over dinner, ordeal though her father's jubilation must have been. Immediately after dinner she and Kevin had departed from the hotel with the declared intention of exploring other scenes of gaiety. Kevin had managed to make his peace with her earlier in the afternoon; he'd brought her into town this evening in our coupé, loaned him for that exact purpose.

In any event, Dorothy was not the ghost at the feast, although she alone might have been justified in behaving as such.

I could find no justification for Brad. If he couldn't reconcile himself to the diminished place he'd henceforth occupy in Rosamond's concern, if the immeasurable benefits her marriage would bring in its wake couldn't offset his sense of personal loss, bereavement . . .

"Elizabeth, will you take a chance?"

Only one person could pronounce chance in that way. It fell agreeably on my ears. Amos, making a bobbing little bow, seemed a veritable angel of deliverance.

His own willingness to take a chance ebbed, unfortunately, as we threaded our way through the crowded lounge. "Perhaps if we watched for a moment I could get the hang of it," he said, steering me to a small table on the opposite side of the dance floor. "I don't want to make a show of myself."

This I could understand; Susan was dancing with a tall good-looking young Westerner; they were as skillful as professionals.

"Jim and I learned this in Colorado a couple of summers ago," I said.

"Jim's good. And for a woman of her age," Amos conceded, "Rosamond isn't too bad."

I bit back a smile. It was not only his interest in Susan that he made ostrichlike efforts to camouflage. What he really meant was that he didn't like or approve of Rosamond.

"The words to the tune help," I said with as straight a face as I could muster. "'Put your little foot, put your little foot' . . ."

Amos dropped the pretense of wanting to learn the steps to "La Varsovienne"; what he wanted to do was to talk. It had taken the champagne at dinner and the brandy afterwards to break down his reticence, but by the same token the genuineness of the opinions that issued forth could not be questioned.

For David he had profound admiration. "This isn't his line of country," he said. "To see him at his best, you should see him at the plant. That's something he's created. It's a tragedy that he's giving it all up."

I could not deny that, in principle, retirement was a mistake for a man of fifty; in this particular case, however, there were new and exciting worlds to conquer.

"They won't seem exciting very long," Amos said darkly. "He's not at all Rosamond's type. I had a letter from my mother the other day—" He broke off.

Rosamond's beauty and glamour alone would be enough to make her suspect in the eyes of any New Englander, I reflected, ashamed of the curiosity his sudden putting on of the brakes had aroused. What were his own future plans? I asked.

"Oh, I'm going to stay on in Ohio," Amos said. The pottery business fascinated him; that had been his reason for taking the job with David. And he'd been offered an excellent position by the putative new owners. Which absolved him from any selfish reason for deploring David's retirement. Except for its indirect result of affording Susan a social launching in New York, I amended as the music stopped and Susan turned to smile mischievously over her shoulder.

"How do you like our little Potemkin village tonight, Amos?" she said so casually it was hard to remember she'd had to look it up in the encyclopedia.

Jim escorted Rosamond back to the large table across the lounge, then went around to seat himself beside Mary.

Mary was in gala mood as well as in gala attire tonight; a midnight blue dress she'd made herself, and a small matching hat beneath which her hair seemed uniformly blonde. . . . I felt I knew the exact moment when she'd vanquished the superstitious fear of the morning that something still might happen, the pot of gold prove but another mirage. David had told her, apropos of the midday meal Mrs. Pritchett had spent hours in preparing, "Next summer we'll get a professional cook for the ranch; then you'll have lots of free time."

The orchestra was beginning an even livelier tune. Amos surprised me by rising. "Although I'm afraid you'll have to put up with my own stuffy style."

He had not exaggerated, I found when we were on the dance floor. Impervious alike to the beat of the music and the example set by the other couples, he did little more than walk, sedately, unrhythmically. . . .

A hand fell on my shoulder. The next thing I knew Amos had relinquished me, although with an expression of unutterable distaste, to Spike Noland.

The cowboy stomp was the local name for the exuberant dance into which he swung me. I'd whirled only a few times when Jim cut in, his face like a thundercloud.

Rage almost choked him. "I thought you had more sense!" he said after Spike had disappeared.

I might have said I'd been taken by surprise; I might also have said that the joy I would otherwise have derived from the cavorting itself had been marred by the horsy smell that clung to Spike's wine-red silk shirt. I said nothing, savoring the puerile delight of masquerading as a flibbertigibbet on whom a husband must keep a watchful eye.

Then as I looked up, we both laughed; Jim's arm tightened around my waist.

We stayed on the dance floor until the orchestra itself disappeared to free the stage for a troupe of hillbilly singers. An auspicious time, I decided, to retreat to the ladies' dressing room.

As I opened the door, I saw Dorothy's tall slim figure. She was facing the mirror, carelessly applying powder to her flushed cheeks. I'd thought earlier that the silk dress of clear turquoise-blue she was wearing tonight was the most becoming outfit I'd ever seen her wear. I now realized, viewing her apart from the eclipsing competition of Rosamond and Susan, that Dorothy was potentially a very good-looking girl.

"That powder's too light, now that you have such a wonderful tan," I heard myself saying.

She jerked her head around. She did not, however, snap at me.

"Try this," I was encouraged to suggest, opening my compact and putting it on the glass-topped table in front of her. "I've had to buy three different lots since I've been out here."

She hesitated. Then as I went ahead, combing my hair, applying lipstick, she wiped off the light powder with a linen handkerchief, dipped her powder puff into my supply and tentatively brushed it over her nose.

"It does look better," she said.

And although scarcely effusive, I was shocked to realize that it was closer to friendliness than any other comment she'd made to me during our acquaintance of almost two weeks.

Primarily the fault was mine. I was not only older in years, I had children of my own. Moreover, I'd been so facile in my academic sympathy for the poor girl, so lacking in any concrete expression of it.

I could hardly say out loud, however, "I don't wonder you're so keyed up tonight; I don't wonder you drank so much champagne at dinner. And I admire you all the more for setting your father free because I understand just how you fccl about Rosamond."

The most I could do was to give a tender of good will in the *lingua Franca* of all womankind.

"You look pretty as a picture now," I said.

If need be, I'd joyfully have stretched the truth much farther when I saw Dorothy's eyes widen in incredulity, then crinkle into a shy embarrassed smile of unalloyed delight that made me acutely homesick for my two-and-a-half-year-old daughter.

When I next glanced at Dorothy, I found that her uneasiness had returned, although not her hostility. With an odd, almost furtive air she opened her inappropriately large purse of fringed white buckskin, took a long time replacing compact and comb. When finally she glanced up, her expression was troubled.

"Elizabeth," she began impulsively, "do you think Dad will really be . . ."

Her lips closed in a tight line. The door was opening, several strange women were coming in.

And although I went outside when Dorothy did, the noise and bustle of the corridors made further confidences impossible.

Nor was there any opportunity for private talk after we'd rejoined her father's party. Everyone else except Brad was seated at the table.

Brad had gone on a scouting expedition, it developed. When he reappeared, he shook his dark head in negation.

"No soap," he told Rosamond. "I've canvassed every reliable citizen in town and every one of them denies knowing anything. So I guess we'll have to skip it."

Rosamond was instantly on her feet. "Not until I've seen what I can do." She laughed. "Perhaps it's the unreliable citizens who'd be helpful."

She went directly out into the bar; her bright dress making her progress easy to follow. Now that she was so elegantly attired, I was struck even more forcibly than on the evening of her arrival two Saturdays ago, by the camaraderie with which she exchanged lingering greetings with one rough-looking customer after another. None of them was known to me; nor when Rosamond returned, a triumphant smile curving her lips, did she give any indication as to which one had imparted the prized information.

"Let's quietly get our wraps and say good night, as if we're leaving for the ranch," she said, amusement bubbling over.

Outside in the crisp cold air she led the way across to the parking lot. But when we were all assembled there she explained that this was just a blind; we would have to proceed on foot.

"It's all very hush-hush, like the old speakeasy days."

Brad said abruptly, "I think it's a mistake. I think we ought actually to go home."

"Oh, Dad!" Susan protested.

Mary's initial surprise at Brad's objecting to any project on which Rosamond had set the seal of approval gave way to distress as she studied his face. The moonlight was as revealing as day.

"You look tired," she said. "You and I can go on home."

"I'm not in the least tired!" he snapped. "I have no intention of going home until everyone else does. I just think it's a damn-fool idea."

He turned to his cousin, enveloped in a warm dark coat I envied, having brought only a light jacket. There was no irritability in his voice; there was unmistakable appeal. "Rosie, you don't really want to go to some clip joint, do you?"

"Everyone wants to go," she said with an all but imperceptible inclination of her head toward David.

Before we'd sat down to dinner David had made a little speech to explain the place cards. He and Rosamond had motored into town well in advance of the rest of us, so as to add the finishing touches. This was an occasion for celebration such as he had never before experienced, he declared. It was to be the kind of old-time Saturday night spree he'd always associated with the wide-open West. Therefore a session of gambling must be included.

"As a favor to me," he'd said. "You'll find your tickets of admission in these envelopes."

Each envelope had contained ten crisp ten-dollar bills.

David knew Jackson was not a wide-open town, that gambling was illegal in Wyoming. This had not deterred him.

"Okay," Brad now said after a long moment, as if his indebtedness to David were already a heavy burden on his spirit, *"Avanti Savoia.* Forward march."

12

The march on which Rosamond led us was circuitous indeed, bypassing the busy shopping center, skirting the more populated residential district, then doubling back to an intersection of untraveled country roads, scarcely five blocks as the crow flies, from our starting point.

"There it is," she said gaily, nodding toward an unlighted building that looked like an abandoned warehouse. "Just as advertised. Now if I have the proper password . . ."

"We can all be prepared to be fleeced, and like it," Jim said, his tone light but his expression serious. Congenitally averse to giving unasked-for advice, he ostensibly addressed himself just to me. "One lesson I learned in my misspent youth was to expect to be rooked in a place of this sort, and to have the sense to keep quiet when it happens."

Rosamond inclined her dark head in agreement, the brilliant earrings almost touching the high collar of her dark coat. "As David said earlier, just regard whatever you spend as a ticket to the theater."

There was a distinctly theatrical flavor to the preliminaries; after she'd pushed the electric bell at the back door of the warehouse a prescribed number of times, it was opened a mere cautious inch until she said demurely, "We'd like to see the cold storage plant."

This did the trick. We were admitted; allowed to descend a flight of wooden steps into a smallish cellar lighted by a dangling electric bulb. The man who'd admitted us, nondescript save for the pallor of his face and hands, pressed another bell.

Almost at once a door swung open into a noisy smoke-filled room, rectangular in shape, containing some forty or more men and women. Chiefly prosperous tourists, judging from their clothes, with a sprinkling of ersatz cowboys.

A dapper man in a bright blue suit and black shirt welcomed us with the artificial cordiality of the official greeter. "Just make yourselves at home, folks; and whenever you get thirsty, give the high sign to Bill down there."

With an astonishingly flexible thumb he indicated the well-stocked bar halfway down one long wall, presided over by a veritable giant of a white-coated attendant whose clownish grin seemed painted on his face.

"High class clip joint," Jim murmured, helping me off with my jacket. "Free liquor. Watch your eyeteeth." Aloud he said, "What's your game going to be?"

I had no need to ask his choice, having seen his gaze travel to the far corner where a quiet, exclusively male group was seated around a poker table. Mary had made a beeline toward the crap game but I'd never mastered even its vocabulary. The roulette table was surrounded.

A little shamefacedly I said, "Blackjack." This at least I understood, although we called it twenty-one at the ranch; moreover five of the six high stools in the semicircle facing the amiably smiling young dealer were unoccupied. His sole customer was a local character with the long, mournful face of a moose, whose bow tie and medium-brimmed Stetson, well on the back of his greying head, were quite shabby. Reassuringly so to me.

Nevertheless Jim lingered. Then the other timid souls drifted over, and he felt free to leave.

I came close to laughing out loud when we were seated; Susan at my left, Kevin at my right, Dorothy just beyond him, and Amos on the other side of Susan. We might just as well have skipped all the rigamarole and gone home for one of our friendly sessions. This was about as sinister as playing Scrabble with Johnny.

The round-faced young dealer politely introduced himself as Steve, explained that the lowest chip in use was a silver dollar, exchanged our respective bills for a supply of silver dollars, and seemed more than pleased by learning that none of us intended to bet more than the minimum.

"That sure is a break for me, I'm just about bust." Ruefully he glanced at the stack of black chips on the green baize in front of the lugubrious outsider. "Each one of them's worth five simoleons. And he says his name is just plain Jones."

"Well, it is, too," Susan said, leaning forward. "Hello, Mr. Jones."

The mournful face was raised briefly in token of recognition, then with both of his thin knobby hands Mr. Jones began making two piles of his winnings.

With almost unbroken regularity he continued to win. Even when he split a pair, thereby doubling his bet, he usually won twice over.

"I won't be eating for a week," Steve lamented, again scooping in our silver and sliding over four times its worth in black chips to Mr. Jones.

The initial entertainment value of the surroundings was wearing extremely thin so far as I was concerned. Only three dollars remained of the twenty-five I'd decided to risk at this table; I bet them all. 'This is my last try," I said, cutting the pack, more than willing to quit my place and have a look around.

The two cards dealt me were the ace and the king of spades. Blackjack, in short, paying off five to one.

Mr. Jones, who'd lost on this round, stuffed his chips into various pockets, abjectly got up and ambled off.

Having made sure he was beyond hearing, Susan said, "He's probably made more money tonight than he usually makes in a year. He's supposed to be a carpenter but he's too shiftless to work. I don't see how he could even get into this place, let alone buy five-dollar chips."

Steve's upraised arm had attracted the attention of the bartender, who promptly wended his way through the crowd.

"Scotch, rye, bourbon?"

Thirsty after the champagne at dinner, I asked for a glass of soda; Susan ordered a Coke. Dorothy, who'd been sitting like an automaton, not speaking beyond a mechanical "Hit me" or "Stand," said with a defiant air, "Scotch, please." Amos and Kevin said they'd have the same,

"Rye, for the poor old dealer," said the round-faced young Steve.

I saw only the rather grimy white sleeve and huge hand of the bartender when he returned, placing the tumblers on the table. He'd also brought me a Coke, I assumed, until I'd tasted the dark liquid, and almost choked. It was straight rye, undiluted save for a negligible bit of ice.

As I hurriedly put the glass down and searched for a handkerchief, the official greeter opened the door to admit four newcomers; two men and two flashily and expensively dressed women, wearing platinum mink stoles over slack suits, one red and the other green. Rings glittered on their hands.

"That's for baby!" the older one exclaimed, opening a huge red alligator purse as she hastened toward the roulette wheel.

A familiar drawling voice almost in my ear jerked my head around.

"This looks like old home week."

Spike Noland had paused beside Dorothy. Her face flushed almost the wine-red of his silk shirt.

I'd been so fascinated by the strangers I'd not seen him enter in their wake. That he had met up with them in the restaurant where they'd had dinner, and arranged to escort them here, became apparent from the fulsome gratefulness the more comely woman lingered to express.

After she'd followed the two men toward the bar, Spike settled his wide hat farther back on his handsome head and seated himself on the vacant stool beside Dorothy. She tried to lift her drink but her hand shook so hard she put it down untouched.

He picked it up, drained it. "I need that more than you do, honey."

This I doubted. Clearly he'd already drunk an injudicious amount. Clearly too he was a familiar figure to our ostensibly guileless dealer; Spike would get a percentage, probably, of whatever sums might be lost by the couples he'd brought in. Shill was the term.

The role of shill accorded perfectly with his record. It was easy to imagine his expert appraisal of the probable wealth of visitors in town, managing to get into conversation with those most likely to spend freely, then eventually offering to show them the hot spots.

When I turned my attention to the table, Steve had raked in my money and Susan's and was preparing to rake in Amos Landry's.

"Oh, no," Amos said, spreading out his cards to show their total count of twenty. "You had only nineteen."

"Well, what do you know!" Steve laughed, took a silver dollar from the drawer and rolled it over. "I never was any good at arithmetic."

Amos had absent-mindedly emptied the tumbler of whiskey placed beside him; and perhaps he'd not taken Jim's warning seriously.

"Your arithmetic is excellent when the advantage is with you," he said, his Boston-Harvard accent somehow doubling the insult. "Quite on a par with your dealing from the bottom of the pack."

Steve's smile remained unchanged; his right hand disappeared beneath the table.

I could feel Kevin brace himself in preparation for a fight.

Steve's hand was empty when he raised it; imperturbably he began shuffling the cards.

Spike flung back the challenge, his dark eyes glinting with malice, his drawl exaggerated. "You're not in the land of baked beans now, Amos; you're out where men are men."

Amos said, "'Mr. Landry' when you speak to me."

That's torn it, I thought, having seen the small silver-mounted pistol in Spike's belt; knowing that even when sober his vanity was of pathological proportions.

Not daring to move or to utter a sound, I saw Steve's eyes glance upward, then travel significantly toward the troublemaker. A second later the white-coated arm was again thrust forward, a fresh drink placed beside Amos.

"Looks like you was having a run of bad luck," Bill, the bartender, said. "Or else somebody's not treating you right. I'm going to watch this here dealer."

It was a good act. And Bill looked so precisely like a big kindhearted dolt, close to being a simpleton, as to carry conviction.

Making no secret of his relief at finding an ally, even in this unlikely figure, Amos bet his remaining four dollars, then picked up the glass and drank.

Before the deal was completed he was sliding off the stool, asking thickly to be excused.

The bartender-cum-bouncer half carried him to the door. Kevin and Susan were there by the time its bolts were drawn; one on either side of Amos, they managed to take over his support.

I'd risen automatically; now as the door closed behind them I no less automatically made my way directly toward the poker table. Jim's back was to the room; trying to catch his eye I caught instead the cold eye of a man beside him, whose stack of chips was appreciably less high.

"I'd like a new deal all around," he said, "after the lady has found a place to sit down."

Jim glanced around; when he saw I was the lady being tacitly accused of serving as a confederate, his lips twitched.

"I'm more than ready to go home," I said, striving to convey genuine urgency; sounding only like a nagging wife.

"Be with you soon."

All action had been suspended awaiting my departure. I retreated toward the crap table; only Mary's blue hat was visible. She was in the front row of the crowd, talking coaxingly to the dice.

Rosamond was seated at the roulette table, David standing behind her, Brad nearby, arms folded across his chest.

Bets were being placed; at the last instant a thin knobby hand reached across the board and placed a pile of silver dollars on number 19. It was the hand of Mr. Jones, the shiftless carpenter. The ball spun, gained speed, then slowed; amid a great clamor of concerted disappointment, it dropped finally into 19. At another time I might have been amused to realize Mr. Jones was window dressing, sucker bait. If he could win, anyone could win; so the gullible would argue, as I had argued.

I glanced toward the blackjack table. The seats were again filled; the blonde, younger woman in the mink stole was sliding diamond bracelets up and down one arm as she carried on a conversation with Spike, ignoring Dorothy, seated between them.

Brad had become aware of my hovering distraught presence.

"Where did the others go?" he said.

Conscious that every word could be overheard,

I was careful not to say Amos had apparently been given a Mickey Finn, that being the way men were men in this dive; I said Amos hadn't felt well and Susan and Kevin had left with him.

I added, "So I wondered if the rest of us ought not be on our way, since they have no means of transportation, as you know."

The glaring untruth of this statement jolted Brad. He looked searchingly at me, then presumably convinced of my sobriety, fell into line with greater quickness of wit than I'd dared count on.

"No, they'll be stranded, poor kids. I'll round up the rest." This was not easy. Rosamond laughingly refused to leave the roulette table until she'd lost her last dollar; Mary was loath to quit until she'd won back her original stake. And even after Brad had departed with them, Jim and Dorothy remained to be collected. Jim, as I was to learn later, had properly construed my tone, but had been unable to leave precipitately without risking serious unpleasantness.

Meanwhile David had got my light jacket and Dorothy's polo coat from the improvised cloakroom.

"I'm not ready to go yet," she told him, without moving.

"I'm afraid you'll have to; everyone else is." Jim was making his way toward us.

"Spike can bring me."

David's surprise rendered him speechless. Friendly though his greeting to the wrangler a moment earlier, he now plainly viewed him with abhorrence as an escort for his daughter.

"No'm," Spike told her his tone that of the respectful employee it suited him on occasion to impersonate, his swift glance at her one of warning. "No'm; don't know when I'll be starting back. You run along now with your pappy like a good girl."

More like a reluctant Trilby, compelled to obey yet hating to leave him with the diamond-braceletted blonde, Dorothy got slowly to her feet, then almost snatched her coat from her father's hands.

When we were outside in the relatively freezing open air, she stayed close to Jim, small comfort though it was to prove.

"How did you come out?" David asked him, after I'd relayed my news.

"With my shirt. No mean triumph considering that crew. I've been up against highbinders before but never quite so tough a lot. My guess," Jim turned to me to say, "is that someone in that gang was responsible for putting Walt out of commission. Brass knuckles are just what I'd expect."

Walt, he explained for David's benefit, had been the former wrangler at the ranch. "And the salt of the earth. I hope he'll be back on the job before you leave," Jim went on to say, and I realized he was speaking purposefully. "He's as different from our present 'Lothario of the Lariat' as chalk from cheese."

Dorothy wheeled furiously toward him. "What do you mean?"

"The sentiment is mine but I plucked the phrase from a movie magazine."

"What's its name?" Her disbelief was unconcealed.

"I can't tell you offhand," Jim said, "but I can probably get a copy of it somewhere. I need to buy some cigarettes, among other things."

She insisted on going with him. We had reached the parking lot; both the coupé and the station wagon had departed.

David made no comment; the moonlight was so bright I could see the bewilderment and dismay in his eyes. He turned toward me, perceived that I was shaking with cold, my teeth chattering.

"I was stupid not to bring a warmer coat," I said. "I didn't realize we'd be walking."

"We'll fix you up," he said, patently relieved by the diversion. The keys to the convertible were in his hand; he inserted one of them in the lock of the luggage compartment. "There's a sheepskin—"

He bent over, hand outstretched. Then recoiled as if he'd seen a rattlesnake ready to strike.

Or a dead body, I thought, remembering the grocery clerk's comment of the morning.

Either one would have been preferable to what he saw in reality.

13

It was an enormous wardrobe suitcase, the size of a small trunk, that after an incredulous second David pulled from the luggage compartment.

Such was its weight he had to use both hands to lift it from the ground and slide it back into place.

"But, but Dorothy must have packed everything she owns!" he cried out in bewilderment. "She must intend to leave. But why hasn't she said so?

"How in the world could she ever get this suitcase in the car by herself . . . ?

"This isn't getting you a wrap, though," he said dully. From the pocket of his topcoat he took a small flashlight, turned it on. The sheepskin jacket was wadded up in a far corner, wrapped around an object which he brought out with it.

A leather satchel, stamped in gold: "Spike Noland."

"God Almighty!"

The truth rose up and smashed him between the eyes.

No place, no time, could have been more inauspicious for the blow to fall.

I rejoiced at the approach of a stranger. "Having trouble, mister?" he inquired with friendly concern.

David shook his hand. Nevertheless the intrusion served to awaken him. Slowly, like an old, ill man he put back the satchel and the jacket, closed the luggage compartment.

He opened the front door of the convertible for me, went around and got into the driver's seat, turned on the engine, then the heater.

The benumbing effect of shock, the temporary anaesthesia, had worn off; his mind begun to function. "Don't mention this to her," he said, as Dorothy emerged from the hotel, magazine in hand. Jim was just behind her.

"I'd rather see her in her coffin," David said, so quietly it was not melodrama; it was a simple statement of fact.

He did not speak again until he'd driven the car into the garage at the ranch and we had all alighted. Without protest he allowed Jim to refund the amount of our stakes, but gruffly cut short the attempt to thank him for the evening's spree.

Dorothy seemed oddly disinclined to retreat to her own quarters. Markedly undemonstrative as a rule, she now put both arms around her father.

He stood motionless, as if frozen by anguish, by this turning of the knife.

"Poor Daddy!" she said. "You shouldn't have gone off your diet. Have you got your pills?"

He managed to nod. She still lingered, her wistful manner pleading for some response, some token of affection.

He was incapable of giving it. She reached up and kissed his cheek. "Good night."

Palpably she meant, "Good-bye."

He waited, made of stone, until she had disappeared; then he pulled shut the door of the garage behind the convertible, snapped the padlock.

"Tell Brad to hide the key," he said, and moved swiftly off in the direction of his cabin.

"I wonder if Kevin oughtn't to see him?" Jim said. "He's suffering the torments of the damned."

I found my voice. When I had finished, Jim said what was in my mind: "Suppose it was our daughter!"

Brad materialized on the front porch of the main cabin.

"Amos is going to be all right," he said as we came within earshot. "He was violently ill but nothing more serious, thanks to Kevin."

Only one lamp was lighted in the living room. Mary was standing in front of the brightly burning fire; she turned to face us when Jim said, "David's locked his half of the garage. He wants you to keep the key hidden."

"What's all this about?" Brad said.

"It's bad news, I'm afraid. But you've got to know. Elizabeth can tell you better than I can."

I did not see Rosamond, seated in one corner of the big sofa, until I'd gone closer to the fire. Yet since she too was inextricably involved, it was probably essential that she hear the miserable story.

I began clumsily. "David found Dorothy's suitcase packed and ready to go in the luggage compartment of their car."

"So that's why she made all that fuss this morning," Mary said. "I knew something was wrong."

Rosamond said, "They have to leave in another week; she's probably just been forehanded."

The hint of amusement in her lovely voice was too much for me in my present state.

"No," I said. "No, she's planning to run away with Spike Noland."

"That's the most extraordinary statement I've ever heard." Rosamond got gracefully to her feet. "What in the world ever gave you such an idea?"

"Plain common sense!" I said, so devoid of common sense as to forget I'd not mentioned the clinching evidence of Spike's own traveling kit. Nor had I until now seen the reason for the large check Dorothy had cashed earlier today. "She's crazy about Spike. She has been from the moment she laid eyes on him. She didn't want to come home with us tonight; she wanted to stay and come with him."

Rosamond bit her lip but she could not keep from smiling. "Forgive my saying so, but I really can't see any of this adding up to an elopement."

"Then tell David so. It's the way he adds it."

Not trusting myself to look longer at Rosamond, I glanced at Mary. There was no skepticism in her stricken countenance, but it was Brad who was the sole object of her concern.

His face had flushed an ominous purple. Scarcely able to breathe, he was fumbling with a small square box. From it he extracted a white pellet, placed it on his tongue.

Jim spoke directly to him. "No real harm's been done, Brad. Thank God Dave found it out in time. If all of us keep it under our hats, there needn't even be any scandal. When Spike turns up, he can be given his wages and told to get the hell out of here. I'd be more than glad to see to it that he does."

Brad was breathing with less difficulty. He was able to say after another moment, "Thanks. I paid him after lunch today. But if you'd get rid of him for me, it would be much the best solution."

For everyone except Jim, I could not help protesting silently, seeing in recollection the silver-mounted pistol in Spike's holster. Obviously he'd used it to terrify young Johnny. A man who'd do that would do anything.

I made no audible comment either then or when Jim and I were at last alone. But even after he had fallen asleep, I lay awake.

The night seemed alive with strange sounds. Rustlings that might be the movements of animals but seemed weirdly like the cautious moving of humans. Kevin must be more worried about Amos than I'd supposed; I could have sworn I heard footsteps near his cabin. Then other muted footsteps came more faintly to my ears.

Surely someone was over at the garage.

Only one of its doors could be locked. Our coupé and the station wagon were parked in the other half. The keys might well be in them both. Yet even if Dorothy moved them both outside, she would be unable to budge the convertible. It was so much longer than the sort of car for which the garage was designed, there was the space of a mere few inches at either end.

So I needn't worry about that.

The mournful howl of a coyote was almost a relief. That, at least, was no human being.

A moment later I was telling myself that what I heard on the porch of our own cabin was only the gnawing of a porcupine in the woodpile. Bitterly I repented the number of times I'd let the waitress at dinner refill my large coffee cup. It was torture to lie awake at the mercy of my imagination.

The moon had disappeared. The darkness seemed impenetrable, stifling. Like black smothering velvet.

I sat up in bed, knowing the rapid pounding of my heart was due solely to caffeine. Knowing any amount of crystalline fresh air was pouring in through the open windows. And physiologically it is just as easy to fill the lungs with fresh air in pitch darkness as in light.

On the other hand, rationalization cunningly suggested, there was no percentage in wasting will power on this struggle. Since I couldn't sleep, the simple common-sense solution was to get up and read.

That this would necessitate turning on a light was purely coincidental, of course.

Jim's enviably even breathing had not altered, I found, after I'd donned a flannel bathrobe, then still shivering put a tweed coat over it. The electric current was off at this late hour, of course, but the beams of the navy lantern kept for emergencies were powerful. I turned them so as to shine on the desk, well away from Jim's bed, and resolutely opened a magazine devoted to world news.

In memory, however, I saw the quite different article Dorothy must have read long before this, with its scathing comments on Spike Noland, his contemptible treatment of his wife. The legal impossibility of his remarrying for another several months.

There was a chance that Dorothy had known this already. I could not quite believe it.

Any more than I could believe that the movements I was beginning to hear again were the movements of four-legged creatures.

No, someone was coming toward the cabin. Instinctively I switched off the lantern. Hoping against hope it was Kevin, I unlatched the door.

A flashlight shone in my eyes, momentarily blinding me. "Elizabeth!"

The whisper was impossible to identify. Then I caught sight of the polo coat, knew Dorothy was my caller.

"I need help," she said.

14

Pausing only long enough to hook the navy lantern over my arm, I joined Dorothy on the porch.

By common consent we moved well away from the two darkened cabins on this side of the main buildings, before either of us spoke.

"I've got to get at the convertible," Dorothy said then, scarcely above a whisper.

"Why?"

I could feel the frost-tipped grass like minute icicles stinging my bare ankles, but dared not stir while I waited for her to answer.

She had no way of knowing I'd learned of the projected elopement. Her agreement with Spike might have involved her waiting until the ranch had quieted down for the night, then driving the big car to Jackson where at an appointed place she'd find him waiting. By sunrise they could be well over the state line.

Yet remembering her pitiful reluctance to leave town without him, this seemed improbable. Perhaps she wanted instead to go back into town and check on him. Jealousy of the synthetic blonde with whom she'd left him at the blackjack table might be her only motive.

Stubborn, pertinacious she was in very truth. And the unaccustomed amount of alcohol she'd consumed in the

course of the evening hadn't helped, either. In this altitude, alcohol possessed double its ordinary potency.

I had to incline my head to hear when at last she said,
"There's something I've got to get rid of before morning."

Low-pitched though her voice, it vibrated with anger.

Anger that at this moment was like the chimes of victo-
ry. She must have read the article about Spike, learned for
the first time that he was not free to marry. And whatever
the agony of shame, humiliation, of her initial reaction,
it had been swept away by the more violent emotion of
outrage.

The scrappiness, the defiance, which hitherto I'd de-
plored, now seemed the most desirable qualities a human
being could possess.

Dorothy was a girl of action. Of courage. Quick to cut
her losses.

So you assume, the voice of reason, sounding strangely
like an echo of Jim's voice, reminded me.

Her anger was genuine enough. But it might be the
fury of frustration, blind rage at finding an insuperable
obstacle to carrying out her plan.

Thank God her father had possessed sufficient fore-
sight, even in his state of anguish, to erect that obstacle.

And since he had, since Dorothy could not possibly
budge the convertible, I followed her across the lawn. Curiosity alone would have impelled me.

She made straight for the door of the garage that was
not padlocked. "I'll lift it, if you'll push."

Together we slid the heavy door back a cautious foot
or two. The noise was not loud, yet in the stillness of the
night seemed thunderous. I glanced toward the cabins on
the river side, expecting to see lights spring up. No lights
sprang up.

After a second I followed Dorothy inside, switched on
the lantern so she could make her way behind the station

wagon and the coupé, squeeze into the narrow space between the rear of the convertible and the mercifully immovable garage door, unlock the luggage compartment.

So constricted were her movements it would be physically impossible, I thought, to lift out her enormous suitcase. About to say, "Let it go and we'll figure out something better in the morning,"

I saw that it was not her suitcase with which she was struggling, almost literally twisting herself into knots. She was too sensible to bother about her own possessions.

It was the incriminating satchel stamped with Spike Noland's name she was hell-bent on removing.

She'd inherited her father's ability to keep a cool head even in the depths of despair, I reflected, as she dropped the satchel onto the cement floor, then wadded up the jacket in which it had been wrapped and carefully replaced it.

Her cheeks were the scarlet of poppies when she straightened up. There was a fanatical gleam in her eyes that warned me of the bitterly distasteful next step.

Outside, the garage again closed, I gazed longingly across the stretch of lawn toward our cabin. Jim must still be fast asleep. If he'd wakened and found me gone he'd be up and raising hell.

"Bunkhouse," Dorothy said as I stood motionless, wishing with all my heart Jim would come storming out.

Obviously the satchel had to be deposited in Spike's own quarters. Obviously I could not let Dorothy go down there alone.

It was to avoid going down there alone she had enlisted my aid. This was the crux of the matter. Having seen me reading by the window, and perhaps remembering the kind word I'd uttered earlier this evening, she'd sought me out. Not for any tangible assistance; she could have managed to do by herself everything she had done so far. What she'd wanted, heaven help us both, was my moral support.

If I'd only stayed in bed, resisted the compulsion to get up, to turn on a light! Now that my eyes had adjusted to the darkness I saw that it was far from impenetrable. The road ahead was all too distinct.

A matter of three or four city blocks to the bunkhouse. No distance at all, up to now.

Spike had not yet returned, I knew. No car had driven into the ranch since our arrival. But at any moment Spike might return.

If I were to insist on going over and rousing Jim, he would undertake the task of returning the satchel to its owner. There was no doubt of that. Yet in the process he might decide this would be an auspicious time to wait for Spike, tell him he was through.

Spike had been in a reckless state of intoxication a good two hours ago. Since then he might well have lapsed into complete irresponsibility. And since he possessed two pistols, to my knowledge, I could vividly imagine his reaction to a man's intruding into his bailiwick. A man who despised him as Jim did.

Whereas if I went down there with Dorothy, there was no physical risk whatever. In this quiet the sound of any approaching car, let alone the jeep Spike used, could be heard from miles away. And at the first such sound I would take to my heels. No one would conk me on the head.

Nor, to anticipate, did anyone so much as lay hand on me. The danger was not physical. The harm was to be in quite another realm. Of this harm to come I was wholly unaware. Nevertheless, only by dint of consciously putting one moccasined foot in front of another was I able to move at Dorothy's side down the seemingly endless dusty road.

An eerie sense of being caught up in a nightmare from which I could not escape took possession of me. These were the insane circumstances of a bad dream; two women plodding through the desolate hush between night and dawn.

I jumped, scared out of my wits as a horse neighed.

Probably Diamond. He was too valuable to be turned loose with the others.

In the opposite direction, I saw out of the corner of my eye a fleeting movement, like a shadow darker than the trunk of the tree behind which it noiselessly disappeared. Hallucinations, I told myself.

I stayed close by Dorothy's side, however, when she turned off the road onto the well-traveled path to Spike's domain.

Inside the small sitting room I again switched on the lantern. Both inner doors were open; I shone the powerful beams into each of the three rooms in turn. All were un-tenanted, all disordered.

Dorothy seemed ready to deposit the satchel beside the table on which the sole ranch telephone was located, then to think better of it. She marched instead to the threshold of the bedroom and let the bag fall with a thud onto the floor halfway between the doorsill and the narrow bed littered with the Levi's and cotton shirts of Spike's working days.

Mission accomplished, her fortitude vanished. She began to tremble. She was shaking as if with ague when we were back outdoors.

No shadows, real or imaginary, disclosed themselves to my apprehensive gaze. No sound other than our hurrying footsteps broke the stillness.

We were halfway to the garage when Dorothy spoke.

"I . . . I suppose you'll never want to have anything more to do with me, now that you know about . . ."

It was so unexpected, so piteously childlike. I said without thinking, "Don't be ridiculous! I knew all about it before I agreed to help you."

She stopped quite still. Just as she had defiantly stopped on this same road yesterday afternoon, to champion Spike.

"How could you know?" she demanded.

"Because I was with your father at the parking lot in town tonight when he opened the trunk compartment to get out a coat. You were in the hotel with Jim."

"You mean Dad knows, too!"

"Yes." I could not bring myself to the added cruelty of saying that Brad and Mary and Rosamond also knew, as did Jim.

A strangled sob burst from her lips.

"I wish I had run away!" she cried. "I wish I was dead!"

Shame was uppermost now. The excruciating shame of a child caught red-handed by an adored parent.

"We'll both be dead of pneumonia if we stand here any longer," I said with the obnoxious briskness of the most heartless of trained nurses.

But when my purpose had been served and we were again in motion, I went on. "Dorothy, listen. There's no one in the world who hasn't gone through pretty much the same experience that you have." I did not say, although I thought, it had been as inevitable as chicken pox or measles. "The only difference is, you've had more guts than most people. You've made a quick recovery. That's all your father will care about. He'll be proud of that."

"You don't know Dad," she said with the quiet of rock-bottom despair. "He's terribly strait-laced."

On the verge of saying, "That's preposterous; after all, Rosamond's first husband was just as dreadful a man as Spike," I realized this would scarcely prove balm to Dorothy's raw and aching wounds. Nor would the argument itself hold water; whatever foolhardiness the enchanting Rosamond might have displayed when young, would have no bearing on David's attitude toward the foolhardiness of his own flesh and blood. His visceral revulsion alone would obscure judgment.

"I think you'll find you've misjudged your father," I said, hoping I sounded more convincing to Dorothy's ears than to my own; secretly determining to have a private talk with David the first thing tomorrow morning, desperately wishing I'd acted the part of busybody before, warned him of Dorothy's infatuation.

"The best thing you can do now," I said, "is to take a couple of aspirins and go to bed."

With the sole trace of humor I'd known her to display, Dorothy said, "Not forgetting to brush my teeth and say my prayers?"

"Not forgetting to say your prayers, by all means," I said, and turned toward the path leading to my own bed.

Fatigue like heavy armor weighing me down, I tiptoed into our cabin, began shedding my wraps.

Jim stirred.

I paused, hypocritically unwilling deliberately to wake him yet longing to have some force outside my control wake him. He turned on his side, slept on.

Again in bed, I found myself again at the mercy of insomnia. Yet I must have dozed off, for I was jerked awake by the sound for which subconsciously I'd been listening. The unmistakable sound of the jeep.

It stopped at the bunkhouse. Spike had come home at last. The stillness was complete.

The time was four thirteen by the bedside clock.

When I next opened my eyes the clock hands pointed to nine twenty-seven. The room was flooded with sunlight.

The other bed was empty. I sat up in alarm, instantly remembering Jim's intention of interviewing Spike, dismissing him. Jim moved quickly toward me, fully dressed. He'd been up for a long time, he said; breakfasted before eight.

I saw then he had closed the windows, lighted the fire and put a pot of coffee on the flat lid of the stove to keep hot. Not until I'd drunk two cups of coffee with cream and sugar did I learn that my fears for Jim's safety, at least, had been forever groundless.

His hand tightly over mine, he said, "Spike is dead. Shot through the heart."

15

Mrs. Pritchett, Jim went on to say, had made the discovery.

Returning in the Ford this morning with Johnny, she had heard the telephone ringing repeatedly in the bunkhouse as she slowed down at the bend in the road. She'd therefore stopped the car and gone inside to answer.

The operator said she'd been ringing the ranch for an hour; there was a long-distance call for John Humphreys. Johnny, however, when Mrs. Pritchett went out to get him, was unwilling to set foot inside the bunkhouse, until she promised to stay there with him.

This she had done. But while he was holding onto the instrument in the sitting room, waiting for the call to be traced, she'd glanced into the bedroom. The curtains were partially drawn; she saw Spike sprawled out on the bed, dressed in the festive raiment of the night before, even to his fancy high-heeled cowboy boots. Assuming he was in a drunken stupor, and outraged by what she'd learned of his terrifying Johnny, she'd gone in to rouse him.

He had not stirred when she'd called his name. Furiously she had seized his shoulder, shaken him. His pistol fell to the floor with a clatter. She uttered a little scream.

Johnny dropped the telephone, came to the doorway.

"Oh, the poor child!" I heard myself saying. "What a terrible experience!"

"No, not in the least terrible in the sense you mean it," Jim said. "Johnny didn't see a single thing out of the way. Mrs. Pritchett blocked his view. And she had the wit to tell him Spike was sick and to run as fast as his legs would carry him to fetch Kevin.

"As a matter of fact, there was nothing gruesome for anyone to see. Even Kevin, when he got there, had to turn on the electric light before he saw the dried blood on Spike's shirt. Of course the shirt itself was red. And a small bullet fired at close range doesn't cause much external bleeding."

Thoroughly awake now, I said, dreading the answer, "Do you know who—"

"Mrs. Pritchett, who was first on the scene, says it was an open and shut case of suicide."

"But why would he want to commit suicide?"

"That, my darling, I don't pretend to know. Perhaps he himself didn't know. He was drunk as a lord, Kevin says."

Rising, Jim went over and turned down the damper of the now roaring stove. "Don't get up unless you want to. I'm going to drive Kevin into town. If we notified the sheriff by telephone, a dozen people on the party line would know what had happened and the place would be overrun with sightseers. We'll have to telegraph Spike's ex-wife too; she seems to be next of kin. And Kevin wants to consult with Brad's doctor. Brad looks as if he'd been drawn through a knothole; I'd swear he'd lost twenty pounds overnight if it weren't physiologically impossible. At the same time he's suddenly become very active, very executive. He's down in the bunkhouse; no one else is allowed in."

Jim made an effort to smile. "The old Groton boys are holding the fort. Amos is doing sentry duty outside."

"Amos has recovered from his Mickey Finn or whatever, then?"

"I can't say it's made him look any healthier."

Jim's hand was on the iron latch of the door. I detained him a second longer. "If Kevin's going to town I'll be glad to keep an eye on Johnny."

"The job's been filled. Kevin commandeered Dorothy's services. He has quite a way with him, that young man. Dorothy looks almost worse than Brad. It's a sort of mutual therapy, I gather, having her take care of Johnny. He was sick as a pup after the excitement was all over. But whether he ate too much candy at Mrs. Pritchett's or whether it was disappointment at missing his mother's long-distance call, or ties up somehow to Spike, Kevin hasn't found out. He's ordered him to stay in bed, told Dorothy to admit no visitors at all. You could ask Kevin if he'd make an exception in your case, I suppose, if you want to."

I did not want to. I hated the prospect of being alone, yet after the door had closed behind Jim I could think of no one I would willingly have seen. Least of all, Dorothy.

Not for an instant did I believe Spike Noland had shot himself. But not for an instant did I desire to communicate this lack of belief. Even in the private recesses of my mind, I did not want to face up to its alternative.

So many people had good cause to wish him dead. Directly or indirectly he had injured almost everyone at the ranch. I had not imagined those sounds when I lay sleepless, not imagined that moving shadow near the bunkhouse. Anyone could have made his—yes, or her—way there unseen in the darkness of early morning. Just as Dorothy and I had made our way. Granted Spike's drunken stupor, a child could have picked up his pistol, fired it.

And in all conscience believed the act was justified.

If ever a man had asked to be killed, it was Spike Noland.

In that sense, a sense not uncommon in the West within the memory of Jim's own father, Spike's death could be called self-destruction. It was a point of view I myself was almost ready, emotionally, to go along with.

The trouble was with my mind. Vivid memories rose up to confound me; Spike, on the beautiful black horse, riding up the road that first day. As handsome and picturesque a figure as I'd ever seen. And with a quality of earthy appeal as elemental as the mountains themselves.

A quality that other men might refuse to recognize consciously, yet which unconsciously aroused their atavistic fear. When Spike had merely danced with me last night, Jim's rage had been blind, irrational.

As for David, confronted by proof that his nineteen-year-old daughter intended to run away with Spike, he had said, "I'd rather see her in her coffin."

He had meant it literally.

And he had had no way of knowing that Dorothy meanwhile had repudiated Spike. Had, in fact, been consumed by rage at Spike's double-dealing. Remembering that rage, I remembered too her subsequent terrible despair at learning that her efforts at concealment had been futile.

Where had she gone, what had she done, after I'd left her in that bleak hour before dawn?

It was out now; the hideous speculation I'd been struggling to ignore. I'd resisted the all but overpowering impulse to tell Jim about the expedition with Dorothy, fearful that once he knew the whole story his thoughts would follow mine.

Well, mine were going to be anaesthetized as of here and now, benumbed by physical activity. As soon as I was dressed I'd start cleaning the cabin, preparatory to packing. Only two days remained until we were starting home. There was a vast amount to do.

I had mopped both the bathroom and the bedroom floors and gone out onto the porch to shake the rugs when my first visitor arrived.

Mrs. Pritchett was advancing across the lawn like a ship in full sail, the breeze blowing the flounces of her voluminous white dimity dress; she was carrying a glass of milk.

"Figured you might need a little something about now," she said when I'd thanked her. Since both my hands were full she took the glass inside and placed it on the desk beside the coffee tray.

"Wouldn't you like me to fix you some eggs and bacon?"

No, for once I had no appetite, I told her. "But it's awfully kind of you to offer."

It was even kinder than I realized until she said wryly, "Well, I won't insist. Plain truth of the matter is, the milk was just kind of an excuse. Seemed like I couldn't stand it any longer being by myself. . . . They've taken Spike's body into Jackson."

I urged her to sit down, suddenly aware that she had undergone a dreadful shock; ashamed of having ignored her part in this disaster, stupidly taking for granted that because Mrs. Pritchett weighed nearly 170 pounds and possessed a serene and even disposition, she was phlegmatic, impervious to shock, her nerves too amply cushioned for normal reaction.

She did not sit down; she seemed to share my need for activity, as well as my discomfort at being alone. The difference was that whereas I had no wish to utter my thoughts aloud, Mrs. Pritchett was as irresistibly compelled to talk as a boiling kettle to give off steam.

"Know just how you feel," she said, glancing at the mop and pail not yet put away. "Funny thing how a woman always wants to clean everything outside when she's got things on her mind she wishes she could get rid of."

I glanced at Mrs. Pritchett's broad back as she began scouring the glass top of the dressing table; a less likely Lady Macbeth would be hard to find.

Then in the mirror I saw the troubled expression of her round, usually placid face. Even before she turned I knew she was about to unburden her conscience of some load. To avoid her eyes I busied myself in dusting the various items on Jim's bedside table.

"Spike Noland's death was a mercy, any way you look at it," she began.

My head of its own volition nodded assent.

"I started out from home this morning intending to tell Mr. Sloan he'd have to get rid of him. You see, young Johnny had terrible nightmares last night."

I looked up; a framed snapshot of my own children in my hand.

"He kept crying out, 'I won't tell, Spike! I won't tell!' I'd say a man who frightened a child the way Spike must have done"—Mrs. Pritchett paused to summon words strong enough for her conviction—"I'd say there ought to be a state bounty for killing him, same as there is for killing rattlesnakes."

Again I nodded in agreement, but this time with sharp unease. Why was she seeking to justify an outsider's killing someone who, according to her own story, had died at his own hands?

Tacitly she now labeled that story a mere technicality; the Western equivalent of a legitimate legal fiction.

"Took Kevin quite a long spell to wake up and get himself dressed and over to the bunkhouse," she began again. "Guess he didn't see any reason to hurry, figuring Spike had a bad hangover or something. Worked out fine, anyway. Gave me time to tidy up the place. Nothing left there to show Spike was going to run away with that poor pitiful forsaken Dorothy."

I chose my words with care. "What makes you think that?"

"Well, for one thing he'd packed all his store clothes in a big grip. I put them all away before anyone saw them. And Dorothy, she'd packed up too. Remember, she told me yesterday morning she'd done up her cabin herself, so I didn't need to bother about it? I was glad not to have to; I was busy as a bird dog getting that big lunch, but I did find time to take her clean laundry over. I opened the closet to hang up her shirts and there wasn't scarcely anything left but that silk dress she was aiming to wear last night, and one of those tan dresses she's partial to. Her big suitcase was missing too. It worried me. I knew her father was counting on staying another full week."

"Did you say anything about it to anyone?"

"No. Only to Kevin," Mrs. Pritchett said. "When I was talking to him yesterday afternoon about taking Johnny home for the night, I asked him how it happened Dorothy was leaving us. He was as surprised as could be. Kind of upset, too. He likes her, you know. Well, I do myself. She's always gone out of her way to be nice to me. She's got a good heart underneath. Puts her worst foot forward. I feel mighty sorry for her. Never saw a girl more pitiful. A rich girl, I mean."

The sounds I'd heard in the early hours of morning near Kevin's cabin might not have been made by him. And Kevin would never take human life. His function as a physician was to save human life.

When she had gone over to Dorothy's cabin this morning to make the bed, Mrs. Pritchett continued, she'd found the stove smoking terribly. The fire had been smothered by a charred movie magazine Dorothy had tried to burn. "Had a piece in it about Spike. How he was still married and all."

I looked at Mrs. Pritchett, carefully dusting each toilet article and replacing it on the dressing table and wondered uneasily just why she'd selected me as the recipient of her confidences.

"If either Mr. Sloan or Mary had known what Spike was up to, I don't dare think what they might have done," she increased my unease by saying. "If they lose this place, they'd lose everything."

"Why should they lose this place because of anything Spike might do?" I said, glad that Mrs. Pritchett was in ignorance of their having in sorry truth known what Spike was up to.

Mrs. Pritchett's tone was one of Christian forbearance as she spelled it out. "Goodness sakes, you're a parent, same as I am. Same as Mr. Ferensen is. And he's had to be father and mother both to that poor Dorothy. Speaking for myself, anyway, if I was him and had taken my daughter to a ranch so she could have a nice wholesome happy time, and first thing I knew, she'd run away with a greasy cowboy more'n twice her age and with one wife already living, I wouldn't be wanting to go back to that ranch, let alone putting my money into it."

No more would I. Nor would I, even if at the last moment my daughter had been fortuitously prevented from running away with a creature like Spike.

This however was beside the point. I knew, as Mrs. Pritchett did not, that Brad and Mary had been informed, in advance of Spike's death, of the projected elopement.

And there was something else I knew that Mrs. Pritchett did not; some small but significant fact I'd been on the verge of recollecting. Her earlier comment about delivering Dorothy's laundry had set a train of thought in motion. I could not recapture it. Nor did I much want to, dimly aware of its leading into a murky labyrinth. Yet I felt convicted of stupidity. Some trick had been played, some abracadabra that should not have deceived one.

It would not have deceived me if I'd used my head. This was to become self-evident after the long day had reached its tragic end. But at the moment I was rendered incapable of clear thought by Mrs. Pritchett's comment as she handed me a whisk broom.

"Wouldn't hurt to give the hem of your bathrobe a good brushing. Just come from the cleaner's yesterday, and now look at it."

I stared appalled at the brown border at the edge of the long rose flannel robe I'd worn last night. The heavy dew had dampened it, the dust of the road to Spike's cabin clung like mud.

I felt just as guilty as if Mrs. Pritchett had said openly she knew of that nocturnal journey.

Nor did I find reassurance in the determined heartiness with which she said, "On second thought, I'd wait till I got home and have it dry cleaned again, if I was you."

16

"I'll bring in the rugs," Mrs. Pritchett said tactfully as I began pulling out the deep drawers of the built-in cupboard with the avowed intention of sorting their jumbled contents.

From the lowest, rarely used drawer I took out a navy blue sweater I disliked. A large blue and white handkerchief was stuffed into one pocket. Unfolding it I found my missing wristwatch.

In memory I relived the scene of Friday afternoon; heard again Spike's wild war whoop, the pistol shot; I saw him racing Diamond toward the bank of the river, presumably courting death.

Presumably. But not actually. Diamond had been trained to roll over cliffs. It was not Spike's life, but the lives of the rest of us that had been endangered.

Rage welled up in me. I felt my cheeks burn with remembered hatred.

Drowning would have been too good for Spike, as Jim had said. Yet I wished with all my heart he had met his death by drowning.

I glanced out the door. Mrs. Pritchett was standing on the lawn a considerable distance beyond the porch, one hand shading her eyes from the brilliant sunlight.

The only other person visible on the landscape was Amos, walking in this direction, although walking without his customary elasticity. Large dark spectacles hid his eyes. He raised his hand in silent greeting to me. He spoke to Mrs. Pritchett.

"A Mr. Frank Wilders would like to see you down at the bunkhouse."

"You bet." Patently Mrs. Pritchett expected the summons. She delayed only long enough to put the rugs down on the floor and give me a glance at once reassuring and suggestive of complicity, before starting serenely off by the short cut through the cottonwoods.

Amos lingered. "Am I disturbing you, Elizabeth?"

"No. Sit down. . . . Who is Frank Wilders?" I asked after I was seated in the long porch chair and Amos was sitting cross-legged on the grass facing me.

"The Gary Cooper type who danced with Susan at the hotel last night," Amos said. "It seems he is also a deputy sheriff. There's a great to-do about law and order today; it was certainly conspicuous by its absence last night."

"The trouble you got into last night was entirely your own fault!" I said, my heart skipping a beat as I wondered if I too would be questioned by the deputy. "You knew in advance the gambling would be rigged. You were warned not to argue. The luckiest thing that ever happened to you was to be given a Mickey Finn."

Amos was still suffering from its aftermath; the dark glasses did not wholly conceal the bloodshot condition of his eyes; his hands shook as he lighted a cigarette.

"You're quite right," he said then, with the mildness that allegedly turns away wrath but has the reverse effect on me.

"And what's more," I added, "you might have started a real fight. That would have involved all of us."

His actions had been peculiarly unforgivable, I thought, for a veteran of Korea who professed to have a revulsion against physical violence amounting to a phobia.

"I herewith apologize," he said, "from a humble and a contrite heart."

Contrite he well might be, and certainly he'd been humbled into the dust.

In front of Susan.

There was no need for me to vent my cumulative anxiety, my own irrational sense of guilt, in verbal lashings. Any man's pride would be dealt a solar-plexus blow if he'd cut so poor a figure in the presence of a girl to whom he was attracted. And Amos, who'd tried to belittle the local scene, adopted an air of superiority, must be sick with shame.

Darned good thing, too, I found myself thinking, recalling his remark the first day here, about "characters dressed up to represent he-men." There had been no disguise needed for that tall young Westerner who'd danced with Susan, and now turned out to be a duly constituted officer of the law.

"The truth of the matter is," Amos said as I was silent, "I went haywire when Spike Noland came into that joint and sat down at the blackjack table with us. I don't mean that as an excuse. I don't mean that I wasn't a fool to drink all that I did. I'm just stating a fact.

"From the first moment I ever set eyes on him, he's been like a red rag to a bull."

Only an innocent man would make such an admission under the existing circumstances, I thought Then I sat upright, away from the chair back, hearing Amos say, "Do you believe that a person who has once been trained to kill, might kill again if he were under the influence of some drug or other?"

"Good Lord, I don't know! How could I know? Why don't you ask Kevin?"

"I did, of course. And of course he told me it was nonsense. He said he'd looked in on me several times during the night and each time I was sound asleep."

"That would seem to settle it then."

"Except that Kevin regards Spike's death as an unqualified blessing."

"Don't you?"

Amos shook his head. Even this slight motion seemed to cause him pain. He pressed one hand over his forehead.

"I wouldn't wish him alive again," he said. "But I can't believe killing him was the only way to keep him from running off with Dorothy."

"Who said he intended to?"

"No one, in so many words. But it's as obvious as two plus two. David got the key to the garage this morning from Brad, then drove the convertible over to Dorothy's cabin and put her whopping big suitcase back into her bedroom . . . No, wait," Amos said, as I opened my mouth to protest. "That's only the beginning. A youngster came over this morning in Spike's trailer—fortunately before the deputy sheriff appeared on the scene—with a written order from Spike to collect Diamond. Of course Brad wouldn't let him take the horse. He did get the story out of the boy, though. The deal was that he was to drive the trailer down to Rock Springs, where Spike would meet him. That's still inside the state, so Spike wouldn't be riding with Dorothy over the state line. . . ."

My expression must have seemed to be one of skepticism for Amos produced further evidence to substantiate his case.

"Dorothy had a great roll of bills in her purse last night. Several thousand dollars. And I saw her face when Spike talked to that repulsive blonde at the gambling joint. The poor kid looked even sicker and more miserable than she did at lunch when her father didn't like her birthday present."

Again I experienced the tantalizing illusion of being on the verge of discovery, of almost having the key to the situation within my grasp. Again it eluded me.

Amos was more observant than I'd hitherto supposed. He was also more capable of sympathy. It was too bad the commiseration for Dorothy he now expressed in words hadn't been expressed in action long before now. That went for me, too, which did nothing to soften my attitude to Amos.

"Where is everyone else?" I asked, curious as to the real reason for his prolonged stay here.

"Brad's down at the bunkhouse; David is in his cabin, I believe."

"And Susan?"

"Oh, Susan's out wrangling," Amos said with elaborate unconcern. "She and Rosamond are rounding up the missing horses."

I envied them. Hard riding was an anodyne that worked. The swift coursing of the blood seemed physically to sweep away thought, purge the mind.

Amos got quickly to his feet; David was approaching.

A David I had not seen before. This was a quietly authoritative, businesslike stranger, wearing an excellently tailored lightweight grey suit, white shirt, striped necktie and polished brown brogues. There was no visible trace of the anguish that had been stamped on his thin face last night. Nor any trace of the friendly man in holiday mood I'd known earlier. I had no difficulty now in believing David was a power in the world of industry. My difficulty, as he nodded his head by way of greeting, was in believing he had ever sat here on this porch and told me as one parent to another, that he had promised Dorothy's mother on her deathbed he would always look after Dorothy.

He took a wafer-thin notebook from his pocket, looked up from it to tell Amos, "I'd like to have you take the car to the service station in Moose, have it filled up and the tires checked."

For the first time in my hearing, he spoke to the young Bostonian in the crisp tones of an employer.

"You'll have to get some new road maps, too; see if we can't get out of Yellowstone Park and up into Cody by nightfall. Look up hotels in the guide book, and make a reservation for three single rooms."

Amos was standing erect, at attention; a soldier receiving orders. Orders which patently dismayed him; his fists were clenched so tightly the knuckles stood out like white knobs against the brown of his skin.

He said, "Hotel reservations may be impossible, sir; this is the last week end in August."

"We'll cross that bridge when we come to it," David said, his tone saying, "Get a move on!"

Amos wheeled, started toward the garage. David then turned to me.

Would Jim and I care to go along? he asked.

I shook my head. David's instinct for flight differed from mine. My motive was not escape in itself but an aching desire to be with my own ewe lambs.

The question was to prove academic, however, before Amos had backed the convertible out into the driveway.

Jim drove up in the coupé; Kevin and Mrs. Pritchett were with him.

There was to be an inquest at an early date as yet unspecified, Jim announced when he came within speaking distance. All of us would be obliged to attend. Meanwhile none of us could leave.

And as a formality, Jim added, the deputy had a few questions he'd like to ask those of us he hadn't yet interviewed.

David was due to go down to the bunkhouse next. My turn would come after his.

17

Jim and I had only a few moments alone; and they were destined to become the most bitterly antagonistic moments of our married life.

We were both on edge, unwilling to admit the extent of our concern or bring into the open whatever suspicions we might privately harbor, therefore unable to speak naturally about even the most innocuous subjects. In addition, I was uneasily aware that I'd not yet told Jim about the trip to the bunkhouse with Dorothy in the early hours of morning. In his present mood he'd be irritated, to say the least, by my previous silence.

What had happened in town? I asked to gain time.

"Nothing of any consequence," Jim said. "We didn't get to see the sheriff himself. He's hot on the trail of that gang from out of state that operated the gambling joint. A tough crew, and no mistake."

"So you said last night."

"Yes," Jim agreed, no less dryly. "But even with my extraordinary percipience I didn't realize quite how tough. Neither did Spike, apparently."

Spike had been acting as shill, just as we had inferred. The flashily dressed couples he had brought in while we were there, had dropped between five and six thousand dollars, all told. Spike was supposed to get a fifty per cent cut. He could not collect more than ten. He was helpless; just a small-time chiseler up against a well-organized group of professionals.

"So he did a little double crossing of his own. He tipped off the sheriff, gave him the location, the password, in exchange for the promise of immunity. Then he was caught between two fires—scared of what the racketeers might do to him, scared of being thrown into jail as an accomplice in case the sheriff had tricked him."

"Perhaps he really did kill himself, then."

"You're in good company, with that theory. More than one outstanding citizen goes right along with you. Anyone as yellow as Spike might easily take the coward's way out, they say."

I had been changing while we talked, putting on the white linen dress Jim liked best of my summer wardrobe. Seated now at the dressing table, brush in hand, I turned around.

"Thank God no one outside the ranch knows about Spike's involvement with Dorothy," I said. "Although if ever the unwritten law applied, it would be in David's case."

Jim blew up.

"Do you think for one minute David had anything to do with this?"

"It's conceivable," I said coldly, glad to find even the flimsiest excuse for putting Jim in the wrong, before I incurred his further displeasure by making the confession I'd decided I must make.

"It's an entirely logical, intelligent idea," I persisted.

"It's lucky Walt is still over in Idaho," Jim said sardonically. "Or I suppose you'd suspect him too."

"How do you know he's still over in Idaho?"

"Because I talked to him on the telephone this morning to make sure—"

At this we both laughed and temporarily the air was cleared. Voluntarily Jim told me what else he'd learned from the call to the former wrangler. Walt had declared his injuries were his own damn-fool fault. He had got into a poker game with a couple of strangers; discovered they were using marked cards, commented on the fact. The next thing he knew he was in the hospital.

Other tongues, however, had been loosened by Spike's death, Jim then went on to say. He'd talked to quite a number of people in Jackson, while Kevin was busy about his own errands. The thugs who had beat Walt up were part of the advance guard, so to speak, of the elaborate organization we ourselves had seen in operation. "Spike deliberately put the finger on Walt; he must have had his eye on the job as wrangler here. Of course it was common knowledge that David was coming to the ranch, and rumor had it he was rich as Croesus. Spike might have figured that on general principles, the pickings would be good. Or he may simply have needed a cover job for his other activities."

"But how could Spike have expected Brad, of all people, to hire him, even if Walt was put out of commission?"

"Why not?" Jim countered defensively. "Brad had to hire someone. No matter what Spike had done twenty years ago, he was the only person available at the present."

Obviously a more compelling reason might be some hold Spike had over Brad because of that earlier tragedy. I resisted the desire to say so; Jim's nerves, like mine, were raw; and he seemed to be constituting himself the advocate of everyone I mentioned.

I must wait for a more auspicious opportunity to tell him about last night.

Had Kevin been able to talk to his sister, Johnny's mother, long-distance?

"No; he found that she was on her way here" Jim's dark brows were still drawn together in a frown.

"Well, for heaven's sake, can't you be glad she's coming? Johnny, at least, will be happy."

"Will he? When she's bringing her husband and his little girl? Kevin doesn't seem to think Johnny will be pleased. Quite the contrary."

I got up; I intended to put my arms around Jim, tell him exactly why I was behaving as I was. His arms were around me before I could move.

Before I could speak my piece, he was apologizing for his behavior.

There was nothing I could not tell him now. So I assumed.

But as the import of my first words hit him, his arms dropped to his sides. He stepped back, staring at me as if toads were dropping from my lips. The initial disbelief in his hazel eyes was replaced by blazing anger. Not at my having kept silent, at my having gone on the mission.

"Someone had to help Dorothy," I said. "And you were sound asleep."

"All you would have needed to do to wake me was call my name."

"And you'd have said it was no affair of ours. That we'd come out here for a vacation, free of responsibility. And we mustn't turn it into a busman's holiday.

"Anyway, it's over and done with," I hurried on. "And as things turned out, it was a blessing. For David's sake. It would have looked black for him, if Spike's satchel had been found in the convertible."

Jim's face was stiff as if from Novocain. He opened his mouth just wide enough to say, "And who would have found it?"

No outsider, I knew. And it was to the interests of everyone here to keep silent. The flaw in my reasoning was glaring.

"If you'd wakened me," Jim said, "David would have been spared the torments of the damned. The moment he'd known that Dorothy wanted to get rid of Spike's satchel, his mind would have been at rest."

"I thought of waking you. But I didn't trust you to go to Spike's cabin. I was afraid of what you'd do."

Jim looked at me, surveyed me from the top of my head to the tips of my low-heeled red sandals. "I hope you'll never need to tell that story on the witness stand," he said. "You'd be laughed out of court. The idea of any girl who looks the way you do, who weighs a hundred and ten pounds at most, taking upon herself the protection of an able-bodied husband, would be hard for the most gullible to swallow."

"Not if they knew how irrational you've always been about Spike. From that first day when he rode up on Diamond asking for a job.

"And it was Rosamond's fault he got the job," I digressed to say. "Mary ordered him off the place. If Rosamond had backed her up, Brad would never have hired him. None of this would have happened."

Jim glanced over my shoulder out the open door. Turning, I saw Amos coming purposefully in this direction.

"The deputy sheriff would like a few words with you, Elizabeth."

Jim drew me farther back into the room for a final word. A word that went a long way toward explaining his seeming unreasonableness, but scarcely made me feel less anxious about my forthcoming ordeal.

"I assured the deputy," he said, "that both of us were in bed and sound asleep by two o'clock at the latest. And that neither of us stirred until seven thirty this morning when I got up."

18

One thing I did know, I thought numbly, starting toward the bunkhouse flanked by Jim and Amos: whoever had killed Spike Noland must have nerves of steel.

I was the only person on earth to whose innocence I could swear, yet I was shaken, sickened by the prospect of being questioned, guiltily certain the questioning would unerringly disclose my folly, and in the process do incalculable harm.

Not just because it would contradict the story Jim had told in all good faith. But because it would lead to the revelation of Dorothy's intention to run away with Spike.

David would then be instantly suspect. Exonerated, no doubt, by any jury anywhere. But at the cost of Dorothy's name being dragged through the mire of publicity.

"Has everyone else been questioned?" I asked Amos, not daring to ask outright whether Dorothy had been.

"Everyone except Mary," he said. "David was polished off in two seconds flat. So was I. Susan and Rosamond are now going through the mill."

"Dorothy and Johnny haven't been questioned," Jim corrected.

I glanced up, intending mutely to convey my thanks for setting my mind at rest about one thing, at least; there would be no danger now of Dorothy's evidence conflicting with mine.

Jim seemed wholly preoccupied in lighting a cigarette. He'd forgotten me entirely, I thought, until he said, in the most casual of tones, "Of course this isn't in any sense an investigation. It's just the routine procedure after any suicide."

"'Suicide'?" Amos echoed.

"There's no official verdict to the contrary," Jim said firmly as we emerged from the cottonwoods at the bend of the road.

An unfamiliar car was parked beside the jeep. The tall lean young man who'd danced so expertly with Susan at the hotel last night was standing on the porch of the bunkhouse talking to Susan and Rosamond. Neither of whom showed any discernible sign of strain.

Their horses, not yet unsaddled, were tied to the corral fence. Susan's short curling hair was disheveled, and the entire back of her blue shirttail hung out over her jeans, which indicated a hard ride. Rosamond was her usual tidy self, wide black hat securely fastened beneath her chin, silk scarf neatly tied inside the high collar of her beige shirt.

I could find no fault with her greeting to me, pleased though I would have been to do so. She did not pretend this was an ordinary day, nor that tragedy had not struck. She did, however, convey the impression that the end of the world had not yet arrived. Life would go on.

And although I was still smarting under the sting of her amused incredulity of yesterday evening when I'd told her Spike intended to run away with Dorothy, I did draw courage from her attitude today. She had everything to lose. If she could remain relatively serene, certainly I, as an outsider, could slow my absurdly rapid heartbeats.

"I'm afraid I've been violating the cliché about not speaking ill of the dead," she said, preparing to leave after the tall Mr. Wilders and I had been introduced. "My own feeling is that probably the only decent thing Spike Noland ever did was to remove himself permanently from this earth."

Susan said uncomfortably, "He really was despicable, Frank."

"You don't have to sell me on that," the deputy said. His voice was quiet, agreeable; as Western as his rangy build and expensive cowboy boots. "It's the unanimous verdict. . . . Be seeing you."

They moved toward their horses. Mr. Wilders opened the door of the bunkhouse to let me enter, closed it behind him.

When I was seated, he settled himself in the swivel chair at the flat desk and turned toward me with an expression both puzzled and embarrassed on his lean sun-browned face.

His hesitation prepared me for the worst. He'd say, "When were you last in this room, Mrs. Little?"

I was caught off guard when he actually said, "Mrs. Little, I kind of hate to ask you this, but I guess I've got to. Why was your husband so mad when Spike Noland danced with you at the hotel last night?"

Hot blood surged into my cheeks. The very lobes of my ears burned. I must have looked the embodiment of guilt.

"It was just a natural reaction, I suppose," I said as calmly as surprise allowed. "As Susan said, Spike was a despicable character. I think any husband would resent his wife's dancing with him."

The young deputy nodded slowly. "Speaking for myself, I would if I was married."

His eyes were dark blue in color. They were disconcertingly alert, observant.

"I wish the sheriff could have come out here himself," he began again. "It would have been easier on you folks." He smiled faintly. "On me too. I don't want to pry into matters that haven't any bearing on the case. On the other hand I've got a job to do. There's a saying in Jackson Hole that if you kill a moose or elk or deer, you'll get into bad trouble, but if you kill a man, you'll get off scot-free. The sheriff and I don't happen to feel that way ourselves. Even about two-legged skunks."

Then he doesn't believe it was suicide, I thought. Nor was I comforted to remember that it was not within the scope of his functions to render the final verdict.

"Would you mind telling me how much money you lost in that clip joint last night?" he said to my astonishment and inordinate relief.

"Not at all. Twenty or twenty-five dollars, I imagine. My husband paid David Ferensen back for both our stakes after we returned to the ranch."

This was not what interested Mr. Wilders. He picked up a pencil, added $25 to the column of figures on a long yellow pad. "Do you happen to know who it was told Mrs. Rosamond Conner where the gambling was located?"

I shook my head. "I haven't the remotest idea."

"We don't like crooked gambling out here," he said, tilting far back in the chair, clasping both hands behind his thick dark hair, so recently cut a white line divided it from his brown face. "Mrs. Conner could help us if she would. But she says she won't play the part of informer. Well, it does her credit but makes it kind of hard for us to clean up."

I was totally confused now. Despite his earlier declaration, he seemed far more concerned with tracking down the ramifications of the gambling clique than in investigating Spike's death. Which was fine by me. I could relax.

I relaxed too soon.

The deputy said, "Spike had a sharp plan all figured out for getting himself and his horse outside the state. He wasn't aiming to drive his trailer, though. He was counting on somebody else driving him."

This was so perilously close to the mark, I braced myself for the flat inquiry, difficult to evade, as to whether I knew who had expected to drive him.

It was not an inquiry I heard, it was another statement. "I couldn't help noticing that out of all the girls at the hotel last night you were the only one Spike paid attention to, Mrs. Little. He just came in, danced with you, then when your husband interfered, he went right out."

Dear God, I thought, speechless with shock, *he can't believe I'm the person who intended to drive off with Spike!*

But this was precisely what he was implying. And if he were to learn that I'd secretly visited the bunkhouse last night, even though Jim believed I'd not left our cabin, it might seem substantiation of this, monstrous insult.

How much my face disclosed my torrid emotions I had no idea.

When I was able to look directly at my inquisitor, I saw that he was painfully embarrassed. His dark blue eyes pleaded forgiveness, although his quietly spoken words were those of explanation, rather than outright apology.

"Mrs. Little, that wasn't meant as any reflection on you personally. But I was born and raised out here, and it's been an education in what might be called abnormal psychology. Our chief industry, of course, is dudes. And something seems to happen to some of those dudes when they get out here, away from their ordinary life. I've seen some mighty fine ladies, young and old, go plain berserk over some of the orneriest, most low-down men that ever drew breath, just because they looked good in cowboy clothes, riding a horse."

My lips were dry. I had to moisten them before I could say, "I don't doubt it. Mercifully I happen not to belong to that unfortunate sisterhood."

"I didn't really think you did," he said, with a quick and shyly friendly smile. "I hope you won't hold it against me. I'm in a kind of awkward spot, all around," he added, sitting erect now, rolling the pencil between strong well-shaped hands. "I've known Mary and Brad Sloan ever since I was knee high. Mary's folks and mine pioneered out here, way back."

He made no mention of Susan. "The Sloans have had more than their share of trouble—"

He stopped short; the telephone was ringing.

We both counted the rings. "That's ours," I said then. Unnecessarily, for the deputy was already answering.

The call was for him. At first he limited his side of the conversation to an occasional "You bet." Finally he said, "Yep. Just about through. Shouldn't take more than another fifteen-twenty minutes."

He seemed almost as pleased by the imminence of his departure as I was.

"Seems I can do more good in town than I can here," he said rising and picking up his ten-gallon hat as soon as he'd disconnected. "Not that that's saying much," he amended wryly.

From the bend in the road near which his car was parked, he glanced toward the bunkhouse. "Maybe Spike did do everybody the big favor of shooting himself. We'll know for certain by this time tomorrow. They're going to hold the inquest first thing in the morning."

That was all either of us said until he stopped the car near the main cabin. "I'll let you out here and go round to the kitchen to have a word with Mary. Didn't want to interfere with her cooking lunch."

I was out on the ground before he could move. He had one more question to ask, however.

He glanced at the ancient Ford standing in its customary place outside the garage. "Does Mrs. Pritchett usually come over on Sundays?"

"No; she just came today to bring back the small boy who spent the night at her house while the rest of us went into town."

"It's just a short piece from here over to her place at Kelly," he said, thoughtfully; then releasing the brake, continued on his way.

"He even suspects Mrs. Pritchett!" I told Jim when he advanced across the lawn to meet me. I went on breathlessly, "I'll have to talk to Dorothy before he does."

"She's waiting for you inside." Jim nodded toward our cabin.

I was appalled by Dorothy's appearance. She was sitting huddled in a big chair, shaken and desperate.

She seemed overcome, not by grief, but by terror. The extraordinary courage she'd shown last night, when Spike was living, had ebbed, now that he was dead. Terror had been injected into her veins.

Time was running short. If the deputy sheriff saw her in this condition, in this room, he'd have no difficulty in identifying the partner of Spike's plans.

"Go back to Johnny's cabin before Frank Wilders comes over," I said. "He doesn't know anything about . . . about anything to do with you. He's got to go back to town right away; if you act as if nothing's on your mind except entertaining Johnny, he won't bother you."

By holding onto the arms of the chair, Dorothy got to her feet. There was such suffering in her eyes as they met mine I could only believe I'd been wrong about her lack of grief.

I could scarcely believe my ears when she said, "Would it help Dad if I told everything?"

"'Help' him?" I said. "Why, it would hurt him terribly. No one would ever believe he hadn't taken matters into his own hands."

The words were uttered, irrevocably spoken, before it dawned on me that Dorothy herself had reason to believe her father had taken matters into his own hand. Had, in brutal truth, killed Spike.

19

Jim and Kevin were standing outside conferring earnestly, when Dorothy and I emerged from the cabin.

"Johnny's champing at the bit," Kevin told her.

After she'd disappeared into Johnny's quarters, he and Jim resumed their low-voiced colloquy. Desperately eager to talk alone to Jim, and taking for granted he'd be no less eager, I settled myself on the long porch chair to wait.

Finally they'd finished, were separating. But it was Kevin's lanky red-headed figure that was moving straight toward me. Jim's tall dark-haired figure was striding in the direction of the main cabin.

"You look as if you'd scarcely closed your eyes all night," Kevin said.

"A fine thing for a doctor to say," I answered absent-mindedly. "I've seen you looking healthier, too."

Indeed, now that I turned my attention to him, I saw that in every way he looked markedly unlike his usual blithe self.

And with this realization came the unwelcome recollection of the sounds I'd heard last night from his cabin. He had certainly been up and about at odd hours. Could he have watched that vigilantly over Amos?

"Did Brad's heart act up last night?" I said.

"A physician does not discuss his patients, madam," Kevin said in deliberate travesty of professional pompousness.

At another time I would have smiled. Now I found myself grimly wondering whether Kevin's evasion was for his own protection or for Brad's.

Heaven knows I did not want to listen to this ugly inner voice. Yet it went relentlessly on.

Kevin's outstanding quality was compassion. This being so, how must he have felt at learning that his young nephew had been terrorized almost to the point of convulsions by Spike Noland?

Amos had mentioned inadvertently Kevin's belief that Spike's death was an unmixed blessing.

Kevin might well have had Dorothy in mind too. He had discovered yesterday afternoon that she had secretly packed all her possessions. He had been seated beside her at the blackjack table last night when Spike came in and sat down on her other side. Even Amos had been left in no doubt as to Dorothy's infatuation. And Kevin was immeasurably more perceptive, even when his own personal interests were not concerned.

Mrs. Pritchett had declared Kevin's personal interests were concerned with Dorothy. And Johnny had accused his uncle of jealousy of Spike.

Simultaneously Kevin had exploded. He had a violent temper, when aroused.

"Reluctant as I am to break up this brilliant talk," I heard Kevin say, and looked up to see him hurrying in the direction of the driveway.

The deputy sheriff had stopped his car. Jim got out of it, just as Kevin joined them. After a moment or two the car started ahead. The deputy was on his way back to town, without even a glimpse of Dorothy.

"Nice work," I intended to tell Jim when he came within earshot. He did not however come within earshot; he made his way into the main cabin. I leaned far back in the chair. The next thing of which I became aware was the low pealing of the dinner bell.

I sprang up, dizzy and incredulous. And quite alone. No one was even within sight.

By the time I was ready to start out, Kevin reappeared from his own cabin, joined me on the path. David had been watching for him.

"Where's Dorothy?" he came out from the main cabin to say.

"Playing a snappy game of Scrabble with Johnny," Kevin said. "I've taken their lunch over to them, together with a big dictionary. I don't want Johnny to be alone."

His manner was so convincingly offhand, it undoubtedly would have deceived Dorothy's father twenty-four hours ago, when his head had been in the clouds.

Today he looked directly at the red-haired, freckle-faced young doctor. He said, "Thank you very much, Kevin. You're a good friend."

Brad rounded the corner before we'd gone indoors.

In the mercilessly bright sunlight he looked old, he looked ill. He did not, however, look like a weakling.

There was no trace of the genial country squire in his manner, nor any trace of the unwonted misery he'd displayed yesterday. This was the man who for nineteen years had earned a living in the only way open to him, far from easy though it must have been. In my partisanship for Mary, I'd been in danger of forgetting that their shared life had been no less hard for Brad, brought up in affluent circumstances, accustomed to luxury.

My earlier thought about individuals standing out with stark clarity in this environment needed revision. What stood out was not the entire individual, the busy working human being of normal existence, but merely the vacation self. Which might be the smallest and least significant part of the whole.

Now that the holiday was ended, the essential personality was emerging.

Mary, at first glance, appeared unchanged. She was pouring hot tea into the tall glasses Jim was filling with ice, when we went into the dining room. Her shoulders were well back, her head high. But Mary had no holiday mask to shed. Except for the few hours in town last night she'd rarely been able to quit her workaday role. Moreover, trouble was no novelty to her; she was outwardly armored against all of its manifestations, presumably impervious to fresh disaster. Other than Brad's physical condition, I amended, noticing the concern in her blue eyes as they lingered on his grave face.

She glanced away from him only when Susan rushed in.

"Aren't you going to wait for Rosamond, for heaven's sake? She's got to change, after all."

Susan looked pointedly at her mother's faded blue jeans, the knees of which were patched. Usually Mary wore them only when weeding the vegetable garden; she must have dressed in a rush this morning and not given a thought since then to her appearance. At eighteen, this was a heinous offense; as Susan had made clear last night, impatiently dwelling on her mother's refusal ever to wear any of the practically new, lovely clothes Rosamond gave them; whipping up little numbers for herself, instead.

Mary was not devoid of feminine vanity, I knew; simply, pride was a more compelling factor in her nature. It must be agony to her to know that both her daughter and her husband worshipped Rosamond.

And with just cause. Rosamond's performance throughout all these years more than merited their gratitude, their whole-souled loyalty. Rosamond's beauty was undeniable, I admitted too as she came in, clad in the plainest of white shirts and blue jeans.

"We couldn't find all of the horses," she matter-of-factly reported to Brad, seating herself beside him.

"We'll send out a larger force this afternoon," he said. His thoughts seemed far away. Yet when Susan, to break the silence, presently began describing the extraordinary amount of game seen in the course of the morning's ride, he peremptorily stopped her.

"I want to ask you something, Kevin."

Kevin's head and every other head turned toward Brad. In the hush the rustling sound of the swiftly flowing waters of the Snake became audible.

"Do you think there's a prayer that the coroner's verdict will be suicide?"

My heart skipped a beat, then thudded.

For Kevin said straightforwardly, with the salutary incisiveness of a physician forced to impart the shocking truth, "Not a prayer, Brad."

Brad bowed his head, his lips working convulsively.

The silence this time was more prolonged. Again it was Brad who broke it. Raising his head, he asked Kevin another, and a strangely touching, question.

"You won't let Johnny appear at the inquest, will you? You can say, as a doctor, he isn't well enough?"

"No, I'm afraid I can't," Kevin said. "As matters stood today, I thought it would just cloud the issue, add to the general confusion, if he talked. Not that wild horses could have dragged anything from him, at this stage. But from a strictly medical standpoint, the healthiest thing that could happen to Johnny would be his talking about Spike Noland. He's refused to mention his name so far. There's an emotional block that's got to be removed somehow, painful though it may be."

"But Johnny's your own sister's child!" Susan said indignantly. "Don't you want to spare him all the pain you can?"

"No," Kevin said staunchly. Then he smiled in self-derision. "Oh, of course I do, in one way. I just can't let myself give into it, though, Johnny's ten years old; he's got to face up to the fact that there are evil people, evil things in the world. For his own protection, if for no other reason."

"You may be right," Brad conceded. "I guess I was taking a shortsighted view. There's something about Johnny that reminds me of myself at his age. Except that his mother is living and I never knew mine. Or my father either. Actually I never had any home at all."

"Brad, you had half a dozen," Rosamond protested. "To say nothing of the one I myself laughingly called home."

This was certainly a new picture of their gilded youth, a radical departure in tone from Brad's former reminiscences. But any talk of the remote past was vastly to be preferred to mention of the present.

"There were half a dozen relatives who felt it their duty to open their doors to the orphan," Brad said, taking issue with his cousin for the first time in my hearing. "Your place at Middleburg was the one where I felt most welcome, when I was small. And had the best time. I learned to ride, thanks to you."

Susan was able to prompt him, now that the oft-told saga was following familiar lines. "You learned French, too, didn't you, from Rosamond's governess—the one with the mole on her chin?"

"Yes, I learned a certain amount of French from Madame Picard," Brad said. "And I received instructions in deportment. What she tried hardest to teach me, though, was a point of view. There I was backward, slow to learn.

"Which is the reason I was sent away to boarding school," he said in a sharply altered, sardonic tone. "The best way to get an education is to have rich relatives who'd far rather pay tuition for you in expensive schools than have you around in person."

Kevin leaned forward. He asked what seemed a ridiculous question, "Didn't you like Groton school?"

"I hated it!" Brad astonished me by saying.

I was scarcely less surprised by Kevin's reaction; the barely perceptible nod of his red head, as if this was just the answer he'd expected. He might have been interviewing a patient, confirming a diagnosis.

Mrs. Pritchett's entrance put an end to Brad's revelations; the improvised dessert she brought with her, the remnants of David's birthday cake, topped by canned peaches, quite as effectively put an end to the meal itself.

"Your fruit jelly didn't jell," she told Mary in an apologetic stage whisper.

Nothing that Mary had prepared for lunch had turned out successfully. She must have expended a great amount of effort in preparing the usual two casseroles of hot dishes, but the effort must have been purely mechanical, for in each one she'd left out some essential ingredient.

I doubted though whether any one of us could have savored even the most tempting fare. This was not an ordinary wake. Whatever grief or mourning there might be in individual hearts could not be for Spike Noland. No one here could be hypocrite enough to feign sorrow at his death. If the agency of his death had not been in doubt, there would be no reason for all of us to avoid each other's eyes, to hesitate to introduce any topic of conversation.

Jim and I were certainly in the clear. Yet even our relationship was sorely strained. Before we'd all settled ourselves at the table, he'd told me he'd started toward our cabin a few minutes ago but found me sleeping so he'd not wanted to disturb me. He had said it only perfunctorily, I thought. And since then he'd been sitting silently, looking almost as unhappy as David.

Amos had kept one hand over his forehead during a good part of the meal, as if his head were splitting. Kevin had been watchfully alert, with clinical alertness that told me nothing. Worse, it reminded me that even two days ago he had classified Spike with dangerous psychopaths. And that was before Spike had terrified Johnny; before Kevin knew of Spike's involvement with Dorothy.

If Amos had killed Spike, he'd probably get off scot-free, unless his Harvard mannerisms unduly irritated the local jurors. As a once-hospitalized veteran, who'd been drugged last night, Amos might be exonerated.

Susan I crossed off the list.

As to Susan's parents. Against my will, every unkind thing Mary's detractors had said of her sprang vividly to mind. "A backwoods Becky Sharp, always with her eye on the main chance," the most articulate of this faction had said.

As soon as David had arrived here, thirteen days ago, Mary had instantly won his trust, as well as liking. He had said forthrightly day before yesterday, alone with Jim and me, that in advance of meeting Mary he'd been somewhat skeptical about the alibi she'd given Brad twenty years ago. Rosamond had told him beforehand of the reason for her cousin Brad's living in Wyoming; the unjust accusation of manslaughter from which he had been cleared by the testimony of the girl he had then married. "I couldn't help wondering about that testimony," David had admitted. "But after I'd spent a little time alone with Mary, my first day out here, I knew that whatever she had said, on or off the witness stand, would be the plain unvarnished truth."

My own point of view was somewhat different. Mary's past was not even of academic importance. Even if she had committed perjury when she was eighteen, even if her motive had been ambition to make what had promised then to be an advantageous marriage, she had expiated a hundredfold during these intervening two decades. As of here and now, a woman of thirty-eight, she was a human being for whom I felt profound admiration and respect.

Far from blinding me to the possibility of her having killed Spike, however, I could readily imagine circumstances that would lead her to determine quietly and implacably to rid the world of him, with no more compunction than she'd feel in shooting a marauding coyote. For there was one chink in her armor: Brad's welfare. She'd been impervious to all else last night but his threatened heart attack.

If she had become convinced that it was a question between his life and Spike's, I could not doubt the choice she would have made. Nor could I doubt her ability to act on her decision.

Rosamond would be no less capable of carrying out any plan on which she had determined. In her case, my not unprejudiced reasoning went, the plan would be coolly figured out, nothing left to chance. Assuming someone here had killed Spike with calm deliberation, foreseeing great advantage from his death, Rosamond qualified pre-eminently. She would have erred grievously in judgment; far from any advantage, the result had been catastrophe. But allowing for this fallibility, she unquestionably possessed the physical courage and the single-mindedness of purpose that had been requisite, if Spike's death had been premeditated, due to design.

But what design? Mary might have been so carried away by fear that an encounter between Brad and Spike would result fatally for Brad, as not to look beyond the immediate present. Rosamond, however, was notably farseeing. She would have realized the long-range disaster to Brad of Spike's death occurring on his premises. No one in this part of the country was apt to forget now the as yet unsolved death of that other cowboy, whom Spike had accused Brad of killing.

The only person who had benefited from Spike's death, so far as I could see, had been Dorothy. And I could not imagine Rosamond's going to violent lengths in order to protect Dorothy.

Brad rapped on the table with a pencil to command attention. He had been making notes on a memorandum pad; he now glanced up from it to announce:

"We'll have supper at the picnic grounds."

"Oh, for Pete's sake!" Susan said. "If you must put up the charcoal grille and cook steaks, Dad, at least do it right here, so there won't be all that fuss."

"We'll have supper at the picnic grounds," Brad repeated. "I'd like everyone to be at the corral by six o'clock."

"I'm afraid Johnny had better stay put," Kevin said. "But I can fix supper for us both."

"No, Mrs. Pritchett has agreed to look after him," Brad said. "You can come with Mary in the station wagon and bring the food."

Mary spoke up at last. "How are you going to get there yourself? No sense taking the jeep."

She might as well have kept silent. Brad took out his watch. "It's not quite three. There will be ample time to get ready if everyone pitches in and helps."

He had worked out a careful schedule, read off each name and delegated task with such firm captain-of-the-ship authoritativeness, protest would have been the equivalent of mutiny.

There was no protest. Perhaps everyone felt the same relief I felt at having no need to make any decision, merely to obey orders.

My assignment was kitchen duty; I would immeasurably have preferred to be one of the group chosen to ride in search of the missing horses. But any occupation was better than idleness, and this was to serve a worthy purpose. For once I welcomed the prospect of a picnic meal, eaten well away from the ranch.

Then as chairs were being pushed back, Brad said, "I'll be in the cardroom, if I'm wanted for anything important. Otherwise I don't want to be disturbed. I've got some clerical work to do, some accounts to settle."

Normally he rested after lunch; his departure from routine in this regard was unsurprising; it was the harshness of his tone that was abnormal.

The weekly bills had been presented, yesterday. So he couldn't intend to occupy himself that way.

My next thought was that verbally he'd been settling accounts of another nature throughout the meal; deliberately destroying the legend he'd hitherto taken pains to foster, of a wonderfully privileged childhood and youth. It was all a matter of emphasis, of course. His emphasis today had an all too familiar ring.

What Brad had said of himself just now was what was said in extenuation of countless derelicts; orphaned, homeless, shunted from one place to another; always on sufferance, never knowing the stability of permanence.

As the afternoon wore on, the continuous click-clack of his typewriter, unrapid and faint though its sound through the partition of logs, became the torturing drip-drip of water.

20

It was well after five o'clock and the hamper was almost filled, when I became aware that the sound of the typewriter had ceased.

A moment later Brad came into the kitchen, carrying a large manila envelope, addressed in ink, with a row of stamps across the top.

Did any of us know whether Jim had come back? Neither Mary nor I could tell him. Dorothy, however, was seated at the small table by the front window. She said, "Yes, he came back a little while ago. He's over at his cabin now."

Her sideways glance at me was so peculiar I looked over her shoulder, half expecting to see Jim turning cart wheels.

He was sitting on the grass, smoking a cigarette; Rosamond was seated on the porch step facing him, hands clasped around her knees.

They both got to their feet as Brad approached. Rosamond started instantly in the direction of her own cabin. The two men talked together for a moment, then Brad gave Jim the big envelope, and moved off toward the corral. Jim went inside, but came out almost at once, strode across the lawn to the garage, envelope in hand.

After he'd disappeared down the road in the blue coupé, Dorothy turned to Mary. "You needn't put a plate or cup in for me; I'm going to stay here with Johnny and Mrs. Pritchett."

"Oh, no you're not!" Mary said. "You're going to do exactly what Brad Sloan told you to do. Don't make any mistake about that."

She was in deadly earnest, I saw; close to the breaking point. Up to now no one of us had said anything that was not connected with our respective tasks. Brad had shown wisdom, I'd thought, in assigning three of us to work together. Two is the number for intimacy; add one more and you add restraint.

Mary's restraint had cracked, however. "What's so special about you that you can't take what the rest of us have got to take?"

Dorothy shrank back as if from a physical blow. Mary was undeterred. From what private hell, what pit of despair, her words came, I could only conjecture.

"Some day you'll get down on your knees and give thanks to God Almighty for what you've been spared!"

The blast did not seem to affect Dorothy; it was Mary's own mood it shattered.

She went over and put her hand awkwardly on the girl's shoulder. "But that day hasn't come yet," she said contritely. "I know. I'm sorry. Forgive me. I was your age once myself. Although to hear me talk you wouldn't think so."

Neither of them glanced up as I went out.

Before I'd finished dressing Jim returned. He had gone no farther than the post office in Moose, where he'd mailed the heavy envelope addressed to himself at the Wort Hotel in Jackson, he said. There was no sign of the anger that had marked our last talk alone; there was an impersonal politeness I found far harder to endure.

Brad had made no explanation of what was in the envelope beyond saying his life insurance policy was one of the enclosed documents which he wanted put in safe keeping.

"But perhaps he was just dramatizing things a bit," Jim added. "He has that tendency, Rosamond says."

Mechanically I began polishing my cowboy boots to a gloss that would be gone before I'd walked ten yards in them.

"When Brad was a boy he had a bad accident on a horse," Jim went on in the same impersonal tone. "He was thrown against a stone wall, had a serious concussion. It changed his personality. Sometimes there is a permanent injury to the brain from a thing like that. And if there is, drinking plays the devil."

I glanced up briefly. "Brad didn't have anything to drink before lunch, did he?"

"Not that I know of. But I was thinking of last night. He did drink quite a lot, all in all."

I met Jim's eyes squarely now. "Do you mean to tell me Rosamond accuses Brad of . . . of . . ."

"There's no need to sputter. Of course she didn't accuse him! Quite the contrary. What she was trying to do, was to get some legal advice. It was all hypothetical. What she wanted to know was whether if Brad did have some pressure on the brain that would be increased by alcohol, he would be held responsible for his actions."

"Why didn't she think of that twenty years ago, when he was arrested for manslaughter? Then he really had been drinking."

"She did," Jim said reasonably. "She engaged the best psychiatrist in this part of the country. But before he could get here, Mary had testified; given Brad an alibi. Which was immeasurably more helpful."

All of this was undeniable. And I'd known about the psychiatrist. My argument had been senseless. But I'd be damned if I was going to admit it. I said, "If that's the kind of irresponsible person Rosamond really believes Brad is, then I think she was utterly lacking in conscience in wanting David to buy the ranch for Brad to run. And what's more," I declared, pulling on my boots and getting up to stamp my feet into the heels with considerably more force than needed, "it was worse than foolish for her to let Brad engage Spike Noland. It was criminal."

Jim raised a dark eyebrow. "Feel better now?"

"No, I don't!" I snapped, realizing he was humanly a shade flattered by my outburst, recognizing the element of jealousy that had prompted it.

"Well, just the same, we'll have to be on our way," he said, opening the door.

I stood for a moment on the porch.

Two weeks ago I had gazed upon this scene and called it Paradise. At this sunset hour, the sky was even more glorious. The rosy light reflected from the billowing clouds of crimson on the fresh snow of the Grand Teton was indescribably beautiful. But I found no comfort in it.

Spike Noland's advent had in very truth been the advent of the serpent. Nor had his influence vanished with his death. Never would it be exorcized until the truth were known.

Yet I had to summon physical effort to step off the porch, move toward the appointed meeting place, knowing in the marrow of my bones that Brad's careful design for the evening had been built around the revealing of that truth.

21

Brad was standing midway between the large red barn and the bunkhouse, watch in hand, when we arrived.

I was glad we were on time. He made no comment in words as the others began tardily to appear, yet his very silence, as he glanced meaningly at his watch, was a rebuke.

He himself, however, further delayed our departure until Mary and Kevin were well started on their way in the station wagon. So circuitous and precipitous a way by car, they needed a head start if they were to reach the picnic grounds before us. But this hardly seemed sufficient reason for our standing around indefinitely. Brad must be overfond of dramatizing himself, as Rosamond had said. Tonight he'd cast himself in the role of martinet, and was playing it to the hilt.

The sun had slid over the mountain peaks, drawing with it all the warmth from the air, when at last he gave the signal. Amos and Jim began untying the horses; I was busily putting on the leather jacket I'd intended to fasten to my saddle, when Rosamond's cry rang out.

"Don't be a fool! Brad!"

Brad, I saw then, was leading out of the barn the beautiful black horse Spike had claimed as his own.

Rosamond moved swiftly toward him.

"Better not come too near," Brad said.

She stepped back, consternation in her outflung arms. Wheeling around, she said imploringly, "Can't someone stop him?"

Susan said what everyone must have been thinking, "If you can't stop him, no one can."

Beneath the straight-brimmed black hat Rosamond's face seemed white, her eyes enormous. It was she, I thought, who should have ridden Diamond. Who had intended to ride him. And a superb sight it would have been. She was wearing a black shirt and black frontier pants; a silver belt encircled her slender waist, silver spurs shone at the heels of her black boots.

"Anyway," Susan added, either through filial pride or in effort to comfort Rosamond, "Dad's ridden many a bucking bronco in his day."

But that day had ended. Since his heart attack a year ago, he'd not ridden even the gentlest old nag.

To attempt to ride this spirited resistant creature would be plain suicide.

Which might, I realized, my own heart pounding, be his deliberate intent. The terrible design underlying all of his meticulous planning; keeping Johnny safely away, dispatching Kevin with Mary, the document he had entrusted to Jim for safe keeping, together with his life insurance policy.

A policy that might become invalid in the event of suicide that was demonstrable as such. But a fatal injury while riding would not be put into that category; it would count as an accident. Mary and Susan would have some provision for their future. "The rest of you get going!" Brad commanded. Each of us mounted, rode in single file through the gate Amos held open. There we halted, turned so as to face the arena.

Battleground was a more fitting word. Even at a Madison Square Garden rodeo I've never seen a more hair-raising spectacle.

Brad managed to swing up into the saddle; but once he was there, Diamond resorted to every savage equine trick to rid himself of this unfamiliar human encumbrance; rearing, plunging, bucking.

Each second I expected Brad to be thrown. By what seemed a miracle he remained in the saddle as if welded to it Eventually he succeeded in obtaining complete mastery over Diamond, forcing him to trot docilely round and round in a circle then walk at a sedate pace through the gateway and then stand quietly until Amos had closed the gate and pushed shut the wooden bar.

Nor was there any further overt rebellion in the course of the three-mile ride.

Brad and Rosamond led the procession, fittingly enough; the rest of us kept a considerable distance behind. David and I rode side by side where the road was wide enough. Neither of us was inclined to conversation; we suffered from the awkwardness of having once talked on a basis of rock-bottom reality, to which we could not now revert, yet which made talk on an artificial plane impossible.

Dorothy had inherited more from her father than sandy hair and slenderness of build; she'd come by her singleness of purpose no less honestly, I thought, recognizing the flamboyant flannel shirt David was wearing as one of the two Dorothy had given him yesterday. Then he'd all but ignored her offering, in his delight at the handsome shirts Rosamond had given him. But today, now that it was too late, he seemed all parent; as if his dream of personal happiness had been wholly submerged by his terrible sense of responsibility, of guilt.

I had no way of knowing how often he might have seen Rosamond alone during the course of the day, or what might have passed between them. I did know that when they had been together in my presence, David had given the impression of forcing himself, by dint of tremendous will power, to refrain from looking overlong at her. As if he were afraid of being again caught up in her spell of enchantment, of swerving from the course mapped out by his almost morbid conscientiousness.

I'd no sooner told myself I might be reading a vast amount into such small and insignificant things as his wearing an ugly shirt, his public avoidance of Rosamond, when he startled me by saying, "I'm afraid I was never cut out to be a playboy.

"A vacation is one thing," he went on as if thinking aloud. "But at the age of fifty, old habits are hard to break."

Whistling in the dark? I wondered; and was not sorry the path was narrowing so we must go single file. We were approaching a small river; Diamond was so completely under Brad's control, he forded it without trying to stop and drink. Unexpectedly Rosamond's buckskin proved recalcitrant. Rosamond's nervousness seemed to have communicated itself; or perhaps she was merely inattentive. From the time we'd started out she had kept her head turned toward Brad's, talking without pause.

Brad had kept his gaze straight ahead. In like manner Diamond disdained to follow the example of his skittish companion. The sudden chug-chug of a motor launch caused the buckskin to shy; he calmed down only after it had anchored at the island in the Snake. He shied again nearing the picnic grounds, frightened presumably by the blobs of light looming out of the gathering darkness. All of the other horses shied, with the notable exception of Diamond.

There was no change in his proud high-stepping gait, although Brad rode him up between the two hazardous objects, the station wagon with its headlights turned on, the trestle table on which two lighted lanterns had been placed, and over to a clearing on the opposite side from the regulation tethering ground where the rest of us stopped and dismounted.

Mary and Kevin had arrived a mere moment before us but in that moment they'd got everything in readiness. A red and white checked cloth covered the long table; centered by a great wooden bowl of mixed green salad, flanked by platters of crisp brown friend chicken, deviled eggs and thin ham sandwiches. One tall thermos bottle contained hot soup; the other, coffee.

An hour ago the thought of eating had repelled me; now as Jim stepped over one of the two facing benches to seat himself beside me, I became aware that I'd last tasted solid food twenty-four hours ago.

"It was a fine idea to bring us here," I said, glancing toward Brad as he sat down on my other side.

An almost perfect idea, I amended mentally, thinking without pleasure of the ride home in darkness.

Presently even this reservation was swept away. A distant gleam of gold caught my eye. So much had happened during the past twenty-four hours I'd forgotten the moon would shine again tonight. In its full golden glory it was ascending now, as if from the far shore of the wide river. The shimmering path reflected in the water was cut abruptly off from view by the high bluff of the near, treacherous shore. But we would have all the light we needed for the homeward journey.

Kevin put down a bottle of Scotch and a package of paper cups. Having seated himself directly opposite Brad as if to be nearby in case the old ticker acted up, he wasted no time in pouring a drink for Brad. He then fixed one for Mary, and this too must have been in his capacity of physician, since she never touched hard liquor. But never before had her shoulders sagged, as they now did; some vital mainspring seemed to have been destroyed. Nevertheless she obdurately shook her head; still keeping the flag flying, tattered though it was.

David drank the Scotch intended for her, crumpled the paper cup in long thin fingers. The full import of the statement he'd made a little while ago, hit me belatedly; he'd said he was too old to change; he was never cut out for a playboy.

It could only mean he was not, after all, going to retire from business. This in turn meant Rosamond would not marry him. There would be no town house in New York, no summers spent out here. No ranch for Brad and Mary to run, regardless of any other obstacles.

Only as an afterthought did I ponder Rosamond's personal loss. Her head, not her heart, would be affected. At least this seemed plain to me, aware in every fibre of my being of Jim's nearness, ready to weep with joy as his hand purposely brushed mine and I saw his quick sideways glance that told me all was well.

If Rosamond had been one hundredth part as much in love with David, she would not have made conditions, insisted he uproot himself from Ohio. No, whatever smouldering passion I'd once read into her expression, off guard, could not be fanned into flame by him.

And in any case, the sparks might be nearing extinction. Tonight, her face unanimated, her lovely voice still, her age acquired significance. She was nearly forty-five; and life had not been easy for her since her disastrous early marriage—"to a jockey, and not a gentleman jockey, whose fingernails were always dirty and who was never known to wear a clean shirt."

Whenever I glanced toward her, which from time to time was unavoidable at so narrow a table, her eyes were fixed anxiously on Brad. He had not touched any of the food on his plate, but then neither had she. Indeed, only

Kevin and Jim and I had eaten with any appetite, or made any sustained effort to keep a conversation of sorts going.

Kevin was in the midst of an anecdote about his internship at Bellevue, when Brad broke in.

He had drawn a large silver flask from his back pocket, unscrewed the top, raised it to his lips and held it there long enough to swallow half its contents. Now, putting the flask noisily down on the table, he said with an ironic smile, "That, my friends, was not medicinal."

"Let's only hope it's not lethal," Kevin said dryly. "Why not eat a sandwich with it, anyway?"

"Because I don't want to spoil the effect," Brad said. "There are a few things I'd like to get off my chest, in case I don't have another chance. And I need a little Dutch courage in order to say them. The habit of secrecy is a hard habit to break. You know that, Kevin, as a doctor."

Without waiting for reply, Brad went on in the same reasonable manner, "I don't suppose you believe in mercy killings, but anyone who did, could certainly call Spike Noland's one."

Dorothy's quick intake of breath was audible.

Brad gave no outward sign of awareness; he did not even look at her. Yet there was infinite, healing kindness in his next words, ostensibly addressed to us all. "Though I must say he was about as attractive a man, in this particular setting, as anyone could find. There would have had to be something wrong with any woman who didn't fall for him. Unless she'd somehow acquired immunity to the type."

Whatever Brad had started out to say, had patently been sidetracked by chivalry. His innate sweetness of nature had proved stronger than his desire to vindicate himself.

"I was the one to blame for ever hiring Spike, of course," he began again. "I did it out of vanity. Mary ordered him off the place, so my ego demanded that I tell him to stay.

I wanted to show who was boss. Ashamed to have you all know I was just a figurehead and Mary had all the guts and common sense in the family.

"I tried to hide it from myself, boasting about the school I went to, about my distinguished relatives. But in my heart I've always known the truth—known that the best thing that ever happened to me in all my life, was Mary.

"It's been tough on her," Brad said, quite as if his wife were not present. "She'd cut out her tongue before she'd ever complain. But she's got nothing out of our marriage except hard work and trouble."

"I've got a daughter," Mary said, raising her head at last.

"And she doesn't appreciate you, either!" Dorothy flared up hysterically.

Susan turned toward her. If she'd been a dowager of eighty, rather than a girl of eighteen, she could not have administered a rebuke more dignified in delivery, if not in wording. "This is strictly family, not a free-for-all." Then her voice broke. "I do so appreciate my mother!" she said.

Brad pushed back the tablecloth so he could grip the stout plank, hoist himself to his feet and edge around the sharp corner to the narrow end of the board, from which he could face us all.

Sweat glistened on his forehead. He swayed a little; then recovered his balance sufficiently to pick up the silver flask.

Rosamond said, "For God's sake put that down!"

"Leave him alone!" Mary said.

The enmity between them, glossed over, suppressed for twenty years, was naked now.

Even tonight it was his cousin's words, not his wife's, to which Brad paid heed. He put down the flask, unopened. "You're right, Rosie. Mary hoped I'd drink enough to be knocked out. You see, she couldn't give me an alibi for last night."

David said quietly, "Have you any reason for making us listen to all this when we'd rather be starting home?"

"Why, yes, David. Yes. I have a very good reason. And in the long run it will save you time and trouble. None of you want to appear at the inquest."

Brad paused. He frowned, apparently having forgotten what else he'd intended to say.

"There's nothing you've told us that will prevent an inquest," Kevin reminded him. Hoping Brad might expend himself in talk, obtain release through words alone? I wondered.

I did not believe he would. Nor did Jim, I knew, noticing his gaze travel beyond Brad, as if measuring the distance to the clearing where the beautiful black horse was munching grass.

"I wrote it all out this afternoon," Brad said. "It's Jim's property now. He'll know what to do with it." Slowly Brad glanced around the table, as if saying good-bye to each of us in turn. He said audibly, and it might have been intended for his epitaph, "I've always been a lightweight. But I've done my best to make amends."

He stood quite still, a curiously lonely figure, and in his way a heroic one. Then I bit my lip hard, in anger. For he said in the special tone reserved for Rosamond, "You've done so much for me, Rosie."

She made a gesture of profound distaste.

But for once Brad was blind to her wishes. "There's one more thing I'm going to ask you to do. One more favor. I promise it will be the last."

Rosamond looked directly at him for a long long moment, as if seeking to penetrate his very soul.

"I'm a sentimentalist," he said. "We've had so many rides together."

"Yes." She nodded, slowly rose, stepped backward over the bench.

By the time I glanced again in Brad's direction he was tightening Diamond's cinch. A second later he was in the saddle, reins held lightly in his left hand. With his right he stroked the horse's mane.

Jim it was who thought to blow out the lanterns at which the buckskin had shied earlier.

The moonlight was more brilliant than I'd realized until I stood well away from the table, able to survey the whole shimmering panorama.

Susan and Amos had followed Rosamond to the clearing, stood by until she had mounted and walked her horse over to where Brad waited.

At an easy canter they then set out on parallel trails through the sage, going toward the left, in the opposite direction from the ranch, the opposite direction from the death trap above the river.

There was a roundabout, much longer way home by this route.

It was an almost laughable anticlimax. Simultaneously I felt like a fool for having been taken in; and reverently thanked God Brad had been only play-acting.

There was a concerted movement toward the horses; a general eagerness to be off. Mary, like a woman in a trance, alone remained seated. She did not stir until Kevin and I had cleared the table and carried the hamper up to the station wagon. Turning, I saw that Mary was trying to follow us. The rise was too slight to be called a hill, but I doubt whether she would have been able to climb it if Jim had not appeared and half carried her the rest of the way.

He lifted her bodily into the front seat of the station wagon, then quickly closing the door, stood with his back against it, his shoulders blocking her view.

One arm went around me. I needed support as my gaze followed his.

Brad and Rosamond had turned back. Even at a distance there was an ominous quality in the speed with which they were riding. Their last ride together had become a race.

A race literally with death. Unless Brad, slightly in the lead, were to cut off from the river road, back into the sage.

He did not cut off.

In the unearthly light, Rosamond looked very small as she bent forward over the buckskin. Nevertheless she gained on Brad, got the outside track, closer to the bank of the river. For a fraction of a second they were neck and neck, merged into one silhouette. Then, fleet though the buckskin, Diamond forged ahead.

Nothing on earth could stop him now from winning the hideous race, reaching first the point of land from which the underpinnings had been swept away in the spring floods.

It was Brad's plan, his design, his way of atonement. The ends of justice would be served.

But once more he was outwitted. Once more his cousin came to the rescue.

Rosamond pulled off her hat, hurled it at Diamond.

He leaped sideways. Into the sage. Into safety.

The buckskin could not stop.

Horse and rider rolled over the embankment to certain death.

22

When I was next able to see distinctly, Diamond was flying toward the ranch, Brad solidly in the saddle.

"I'll take your horse back," Jim said, his arm still around me. "You go with Mary."

She was already behind the wheel, Kevin beside her. She had difficulty in starting the engine, then in keeping the station wagon on the road. At best, the road was hazardous; now it was like a roller coaster, save for the maddening slowness of our progress. Neglecting to shift gears, she stalled on each of the several hills. Yet I knew from Kevin's sideways glance that his failure to take over was deliberate; even these erratic efforts were better for her than the total collapse which threatened.

He glanced at me again after we had reached the main highway and were nearing Moose, where the road to the ranch turned off. His nod directed my attention to the half-dozen men running down toward the river. The alarm had been given. David's big convertible was parked beneath the bridge.

Mary saw none of this; it required her every effort to cross the busy thoroughfare.

Nor did she seem to hear the ringing of the telephone in the bunkhouse as she made the last turn of our own road. She stopped, however, when Kevin asked her to let me out.

It seemed part of the nightmare to get out, to enter the empty bunkhouse, lift the receiver, say this was the Sloans' ranch. And having braced myself for a fateful message, hear a pleasant voice say, "This is Sheila Blake. Can you tell me how to get to there? We're at a place called Kelly now."

Mechanically I gave the directions; Mrs. Pritchett lived near Kelly. Someone must be coming over from there to pick her up.

Her Ford was parked in its customary place beyond the garage, I found when I'd walked that far up the deserted road.

The main cabin was dark. Lights shone from Johnny's window. His door opened as I started across the lawn. Dorothy emerged carrying the satchel in which Kevin kept his medical supplies, streaked off like a deer.

Mrs. Pritchett advanced in the bright moonlight to intercept me, with her news.

Mary, she said, had driven the station wagon to her own door, then she'd gone to pieces, crumpled up. "Best thing that could happen to her, with Kevin right there and all."

The ominous wail of a police siren pierced the quiet. The explosive backfire from a rapidly traveling motor boat said further that the search was on.

"Current running the way it is, though," Mrs. Pritchett said, "shouldn't need to dredge the river."

It shocked me; the practical comment itself and the matter-of-fact tone in which it was made. Mrs. Pritchett not only resembled a statue in size but in lack of feeling; her calm acceptance became unendurable when she added, "'The Lord moves in a mysterious way. . . .'"

I said abruptly, "Someone telephoned . . ." Then it clicked. I'd heard Kevin speak of his sister Sheila; her new husband's name, I now recalled, was Commander Blake. "Johnny's family will be here at any moment," I finished.

This hit Mrs. Pritchett in a vital spot, shattered her serenity. She had cleaned the two-roomed cabin assigned to the Blakes but not yet made it up; they weren't due until tomorrow. And she'd promised Johnny faithfully to stay with him until Kevin returned.

"That's all right," I said, more than appeased to find her vulnerable, "I know where the linen's kept."

I had made a second trip to the store room when the sound of a car sent me toward the driveway, arms piled high with blankets.

A green coupé, otherwise indistinguishable from our rented one, had stopped outside the garage. A fair-haired man about Jim's age, wearing naval uniform, came courteously forward to ask if this was the Sloans' place.

It was, I told him. Things were upset because there had been a bad accident.

"To Johnny?" his mother's anguished voice cried out.

"No, not to Johnny."

I moved nearer to say it had been Rosamond Conner. Her horse had plunged over a high embankment into the river. She must have been killed instantly.

"Oh, how terrible! How terrible."

Mrs. Blake glanced down; I saw then the reason she'd stayed inside the coupé. Pillowed on her lap was a round-cheeked little girl with braids, fast asleep. Her name was Constance; she was six years old. They had left Paris three days ago and been traveling almost continuously by plane and car, in their eagerness to see Johnny, his mother explained in the course of gently transferring Constance to her father's care.

"She's almost as excited about seeing Johnny as I am," Mrs. Blake said, able now to step out onto the ground. She had a charming, piquant face; the same quality of warm friendliness Kevin possessed.

Johnny fortunately had not witnessed the accident, I told her. Yet even as I said it I suspected he might have been more upset if he'd witnessed his mother's arrival, cradling the usurper, the unknown stepsister he hated in advance.

"He's been a little under the weather," it seemed best to say, by way of preparation. "He's in bed now."

I had no need to accompany Mrs. Blake. The instant I'd pointed out her son's light, she was speeding toward it as if wings had sprouted on her high-heeled pumps.

Dorothy joined me at the doorstep of the Blakes' cabin, pathetically eager to help. Or perhaps eager not to be alone. Her thoughts were plainly far removed from the tasks to which she inexpertly applied her hands.

I did not expect her thoughts to be following the same blasphemous course as mine. Rosamond's magnificent gesture, her heroic sacrifice, had been worse than useless. Brad now faced an even blacker future.

As Dorothy prepared to break the silence, I prepared myself for mention, not of Brad's tragedy, but of her own. Some reference, even if oblique, to Spike Noland.

She said, "Mary would have fallen out of the station wagon if Kevin hadn't picked her up in his arms as if she'd been a baby. He's so kind. So truly k-kind."

A tear splashed on the striped ticking of the pillow she was struggling to fit into a white case.

My mind told me her crying was sign of health; the beginning of convalescence. But emotionally it was so difficult not to put my hand on her shoulder, to utter words of spurious comfort in effort to stop her crying. I took refuge in saying I'd do up the other room while she finished in here.

Everything was in order; Dorothy had lighted the open fire in the larger room and I was laying a fire in the stove in the single one, against the early morning chill, when Susan came in.

"What's wrong now?"

"Nothing's wrong," I told her, getting up and brushing the soot from my hands onto my blue jeans. "The Blakes arrived a day early, that's all."

"I'll go and bring them over," she said after a pause. "I don't want them to drive the car; the noise might wake Mother. Kevin's given her a shot of something. She wouldn't let him give her anything until Dad got back."

At the door she half-turned. She said woodenly, "They found Rosamond's body—the people in the launch on the island."

Unaccountably I thought, Rosamond's at peace now.

Only once had I seen her not at peace, only once had my heart gone out to her. Perhaps for that very reason this was the memory that now blotted out all others. The evening of Spike's concert. I heard again his poignant golden voice.

> *Build me a castle*
> *Forty feet high*
> *So I can see her*
> *As she rides by*
>
> *As she rides by, love,*
> *As she rides by . . .*

A log had suddenly crashed, the flames shot up. I'd seen tears glisten on Rosamond's cheek, seen her clenched fist pressed hard against it. . . .

It was a picture that was to remain indelible, that was to make understandable the whole pitiable truth, when finally I heard it. When at last the ranch had settled down for the night and Jim and I were alone.

23

Rosamond had not died to save Brad's life. Brad had deliberately, prayerfully risked his life in order that she might die without disgrace.

For as of yesterday, the blindfold had been torn off. He had at last seen Rosamond whole.

The knowledge had been buried in his unconscious mind for years, of course; but up to now he had been able to prevent its rising to the surface. . . . After the fact, I could see proof of his inner doubt in his excessive boasting, his overpraise, of Rosamond; just as he'd boasted of Groton school, which in reality he'd hated.

It was so simple a thing that had revealed the truth to him; in his words, brought the world tumbling down around his ears. So small an incongruity.

And had Rosamond been a scatterbrained, or even an ordinarily casual, unmethodical woman, this incongruity would have possessed no significance.

Rosamond, however, had been notably far-seeing; her plans always laid well in advance, carefully thought out, dovetailing perfectly. Her efficiency was a byword.

With customary efficiency she had outlined the program for yesterday morning; deputized Brad to drive the station wagon up to Moran, assigned chores for Spike to do here, planned an elaborate lunch for Mrs. Pritchett to prepare, mapped out a ride to Taggart for everyone else who was not going into town.

She made only one mistake, one trifling error.

This was the reason she gave for not going with the party to Taggart, for staying at home. And for justifying her spending time in the bunkhouse, should this occasion comment, or arouse Mrs. Pritchett's curiosity.

Jim paused and looked at me. "Do you remember what that reason was?"

"Why, yes," I said. "She wanted to telephone the store in New York where she'd ordered—

Then light dawned. I broke off, appalled, now that I'd found the key, the discrepancy that had nagged at the back of my mind until I'd become convinced of Brad's guilt. "On a Saturday in August!"

"Exactly," Jim said. "But it took me in too. It took everyone in. Except Brad."

Accustomed to devouring the New York newspapers, including the advertisements, Brad knew as well as those of us who lived in New York knew, that every store of any size was closed on Saturdays in August.

He knew too there was no possibility of Rosamond's having lost track of the calendar; not when everyone, herself included, had laid such stress on its being Saturday, the big day of the week in these parts; not when the August date itself had been firmly fixed as David's birthday. Ignorance and oblivion both had to be ruled out; Rosamond not only lived in New York but worked in a shop there that closed on Saturdays like all the rest.

Brad had not only recognized the lie; with sickening clarity he had recognized the motive that had prompted it.

The pattern was all too familiar. It had been established before Rosamond was quite sixteen. This he was inexorably forced to acknowledge, once the barrier to memory had been swept away by shock.

To begin at the beginning. Brad, as a small boy, an orphan, had in truth felt most at home at the place near Middleburg where Rosamond lived. An only child herself, whose parents had been divorced, and whose custody had been awarded her mother, with only school vacations to be spent with the father she adored, Rosamond had treated Brad, four years her junior, as the dearest of younger brothers. She had been genuinely devoted to him; protective, generous, maternal in her kindness.

With abundant cause, Brad worshipped her, willingly followed her leadership, entered into many a harmless conspiracy with her against the older generation. Which in their situation boiled down to the stern inflexible Frenchwoman, Madame Picard, to whom Rosamond's mother delegated full authority while she herself pursued more congenial occupation on the other side of the Atlantic.

For six years, no cloud of appreciable size marred Brad's relationship with Rosamond. Then the summer of his eleventh birthday, he found himself indefinably reluctant to take part in a new conspiracy she proposed. Hitherto she had spent her summers in Newport with her father, but he had recently remarried; she had therefore refused to stir from Virginia. The two cousins rode forth every day, accompanied by a handsome young groom whom Brad instinctively feared and disliked. Plainly Madame Picard shared this feeling, for she commanded Brad never to separate himself from the others. It was as a trio they always set out, a trio they always returned. Meanwhile, however, Brad was sent off alone; a graveyard secret between Rosamond and him.

Despite the uneasiness in his mind, his inability to accept in complete good faith her argument that he'd be far better equipped for the winter's hunting if he explored the countryside on his own, Brad enjoyed the freedom of these solitary expeditions, the opportunity for more daring feats than if he'd been under supervision.

On what was destined to be the last of such opportunities, he tried to jump a perilously high stone wall. His horse stumbled.

A neighboring farmer found Brad lying unconscious in the field, sounded the alarm.

During the long weeks Brad spent in the hospital, suffering from severe concussion as well as broken bones, his fate was sealed. Far from any expression of sympathy from Madame Picard, she declared his injuries were insufficient punishment for his disobedience. She had trusted him, as the man of the family, to protect his cousin. He had betrayed that trust. And the *bon Dieu* alone knew what harm might follow.

Rosamond had not uttered a word in Brad's defense. "There's no use arguing with her," she'd told him in privacy. "It will all blow over."

It had not blown over. Brad had been labeled intractable, irresponsible, in dire need of discipline. A family council had resulted in his being sent away to boarding school that fall. This was his real exile.

Today, a man over forty, Brad suspected Rosamond had implanted the idea of his irresponsibility, so as to discredit in advance any story he might tell in his own defense. But at the time he harbored no such suspicion; he regarded her as his only friend in an otherwise hostile and unjust world.

Subsequently he was to close his ears to the bitter disapproval of Rosamond expressed by the New England relatives with whom he stayed during such brief intervals as neither schools nor camps were open. When Rosamond was seventeen she went abroad; to hunt, she wrote him. To avoid an open scandal, her connections said. "'From the frying pan into the fire,'" they said too when word came of her marriage in Ireland.

The man she had married had been essentially the same type as the groom in Virginia; a superb horseman, handsome in a coarse-grained way; unfastidious, earthy in every sense.

The pitiable and tragic truth was that only a man of this stripe made emotional appeal to Rosamond.

Spike Noland fitted the pattern. So had the cowboy Naboth Bishop, of whose fatal shooting Brad had been accused twenty years ago.

Until this very afternoon Brad himself had never known whether or not he had been guilty; whether or not Mary had perjured herself in swearing she'd remained with him throughout that night. It had created a barrier he had never been able wholly to surmount, destroyed his self-confidence.

Today, riding to the picnic grounds, Rosamond had told him she had shot Naboth in self-defense. Naboth too had drunk raw moonshine, gone berserk. A widow then of twenty-four, she had learned discretion; she had no intention of making a second *mésalliance*. Naively he had interpreted as a serious love affair what to her was an episode; threatened to kill her if she refused to marry him. It had been a question of her life or his.

"No, it was Rosamond's jealousy because he danced with Mary," I heard myself saying, no longer worrying about anything I said to Jim. "Mrs. Pritchett told me about the party. She was there herself. She said Naboth hadn't ever paid attention to Mary until that night. And then he wouldn't leave her alone. Wouldn't let anyone else dance with her. That must have enraged Rosamond."

"That might be," Jim said. "Her story to Brad had several big gaps in it. She said, for instance, that if he'd not been acquitted, she'd have gone into court and testified that she herself had killed Naboth. Which doesn't jibe at all with the fact that she had engaged a psychiatrist and a crackerjack defense lawyer for Brad. I don't know whether Brad fell for her story today or not."

Jim moved a little uncomfortably in his chair, took an unnecessarily long time in lighting a cigarette. The half-quizzical, half-apologetic raising of one dark eyebrow told me he was remembering, not without embarrassment, his own credulity when Rosamond had ostensibly sought legal advice from him this afternoon.

"Let's hope Brad did believe her," I said. "Any consolation he can get is all to the good."

This was gospel truth, Jim said soberly. And went on to tell me what else Brad had said.

Rosamond, in that desperate last talk with her cousin, had revealed such deep and terrible conflicts within herself as almost to shake Brad's resolution, shatter him by pity.

She had likened her emotional aberration to a sickness, a poison in the blood. She had used all her worldly knowledge to keep it hidden; she had fought against it as a drug addict might fight. In her case, though, she had believed time was on her side. Now in the middle forties, she had believed herself cured; charted a commonsense blueprint for a wholly self-respecting, tranquil future. David was the antithesis of the kind of man she despised herself for being attracted to. Marriage to David, under the conditions she had stipulated, would be tolerable, however. And would enable her to make partial repayment to Brad of the heavy debt she owed him.

Jim paused, glanced questioningly at me.

"No; I believe that," I said. "I think she did truly love Brad, as she might have loved a younger brother. . . ."

"Well, if the opportunity ever arises, tell the poor devil so," Jim said. Then he returned to Rosamond's story.

When she arrived at the ranch two weeks ago it was with the belief that her illness was a thing of the past, could never recur.

But on the second day, Spike Noland came riding up the road.

Satan himself might have sent him to stir the poison in her blood.

She had expected Brad to dismiss Spike; told herself she hoped he would. Yet simultaneously she had known she could ensure this dismissal by merely lifting a finger. She had not lifted a finger.

It would be a test of her resolution, proof of her cure, she then decided, to see Spike daily in the company of others, yet resist the temptation ever to see him alone. Presumably this accounted for the long sessions of bridge every evening, after the memorable evening when he had sung.

She took for granted the attraction was mutual. Spike had let fall a laughing word or two during the first afternoon's ride to the effect that he'd sought the job here because he'd seen her in town the evening of her arrival. His manner had shown that he had no illusions about her, was not intimidated by her external, polished surface. This in itself forged a bond, established a tacit understanding that lent zest to their most casual encounters. But because Rosamond felt such contempt for him intellectually, she woefully underestimated his native intelligence, overestimated her own powers of attraction for him.

I thought parenthetically that Spike's experiences in Reno and in Hollywood had probably taught him a vast amount about the vulnerability of women past their first bloom.

Jim said, "Spike's eyes were fixed on the main chance. He probably told Rosamond a half-truth in saying he'd come here because she was here. It seems likely, the way Brad and I figure it, that the possibility of blackmail occurred to him the moment he heard Rosamond was involved with David. Spike was close enough to Naboth Bishop to have known about his affair with Rosamond."

There was no way of proving what was in Spike's mind, but from the available evidence it seemed reasonable to suppose that as soon as he'd met Dorothy, he'd set his sights even higher. His goal was now a dual one. Dorothy had no inkling of the legal obstacle that would prevent his marrying her for several months. He was acutely mindful of this obstacle, though; of the serious trouble in which he'd land unless he could obtain so powerful a hold over Rosamond she would be compelled by self-interest to prevent David from taking action.

He chose the most auspicious of moments to arrange a private meeting with Rosamond; Friday last, the day she and David became formally engaged, the day Spike himself performed the daredevil stunt of riding Diamond over the cliff into the river.

Rosamond had gone to his aid. Unnecessarily, as it turned out. Yet in the few moments she and Spike were alone, before the rest of us arrived back at the ranch, she had agreed to meet him privately the next morning.

This meeting in the bunkhouse was the first occasion they were ever alone for any length of time. What transpired would never be known in entirety. As an accomplished Don Juan, Spike naturally had not revealed his actual purpose in suggesting the rendezvous. He had mentioned Naboth Bishop, as if in passing; said enough so that Rosamond, off guard, assumed he knew the facts of Naboth's death and therefore unwittingly she disclosed them.

A gold mine was now within Spike's easy reach. An inexhaustible gold mine. As David's wife, Rosamond would be exceedingly rich. And if David were to consider disinheriting Dorothy, Rosamond would be compelled to prevent his doing so.

Yet even with this Eldorado in sight, Spike was no less ready to turn a dishonest penny. He had easily persuaded Rosamond to steer David's party to the gambling joint in Jackson that evening. Her little tour of the Silver Dollar bar, ostensibly in search of information, had been deliberate camouflage. Spike's brief appearance on the dance floor had been a mute signal to her that she could now proceed. This to her was merely an amusing decoration of the understanding she believed she had reached with him.

The disclosure I had made late that night, of Spike's intention to elope with Dorothy, had at first struck Rosamond as genuinely preposterous, absurd. She had laughed in complete good faith. When she'd been forced to accept it as reality, she had reeled under the blow.

Her horror struck deeper than vanity, deeper than the proverbial fury of a woman scorned.

As long as Spike lived, he would be a threat to her. She would never be safe.

He must not be permitted to live.

Brad, watching her intently, had been terrified by her expression. This had been the cause of his threatened heart attack.

He had not gone to bed. Not undressed. As soon as the ranch was quiet, he had made his way down to the knoll of cottonwoods opposite the bunkhouse, to stand guard. . . . He was the shadow I had seen. Just as he had seen Dorothy and me go into the bunkhouse, leave in a matter of seconds. . . At long last he'd heard the sound of the jeep, known Spike was returning.

Spike had been scarcely able to get himself out of the jeep; he had neglected to turn off its engine or its lights.

This was one of those petty maddening occurrences that upset the most carefully thought out strategy. Brad found himself aching to shut off the car's motor, yet fearful of disclosing his presence.

While he was debating the question, the night again became still and dark. The motor had been shut off, the lights extinguished.

Spike was not as helpless as he'd supposed, Brad thought.

Then he saw a swiftly moving figure that could not be Spike's emerge from the bunkhouse. There was nothing uncertain in its movements, in the direct course it followed up the road. A figure so expertly camouflaged as to have eluded Brad's vision before. Sheathed in black, black-gloved, only the faint white blur of Rosamond's face was visible beneath the upturned hood of her black coat.

. . . I found myself shivering, unable to stop. I had no difficulty in understanding the course Brad's thoughts had followed; his decision not to enter Spike's cabin, not to have the knowledge of his own eyes confirm his moral certainty.

There was one crucial point I could not understand, however.

"That last ride Brad suggested this evening," I said. "That race. Suppose he had been the one to go into the river, instead of Rosamond. How could he, knowing everything, have taken such a hideous gamble?"

Jim shook his head. "Not as hideous, not as much of a gamble, as it might have seemed. Remember, Diamond's a trick horse. He'd gone off that same bluff, into the Snake, with Spike the other afternoon, and come up safely. Brad had all of this in mind. . . . And to make certain, in case there should be a slip-up, he'd written out all the salient facts. That was the most important of the documents in that big envelope he gave me this afternoon. He told Rosamond he'd put it all down in black and white."

I was still shivering.

"I'll get some more wood for the stove," Jim said.

When he came back inside, he said that Kevin's light was still on.

A moment later Kevin himself appeared at the door.

"Is anything wrong with Johnny?" I asked.

"Nothing I can put a name to. Oh, he's fast asleep. But he didn't show any great joy at seeing his mother." Kevin shook his carroty head, bemused. "Sheila said he had very little to say to her. And of course he's practically not opened his mouth to me since Spike died.

"However, what I came over to ask was whether you wouldn't like a mild sedative? This has been a hell of a day."

"Yes, on both counts," I fervently agreed.

24

Not fully awake even after I'd washed my face and donned a bathrobe, I apologized to Susan for having slept until the disgraceful hour of eleven thirty, thereby putting her to all this trouble.

"No trouble at all," she said as I sat down at the desk on which she'd placed a carefully laid breakfast tray. "Good practice, too," she puzzled me by adding. "I made Mother have a tray too. She says she feels fine, but she'd say it anyway."

Yes, I thought, she would. And so would Susan. I glanced up at her, standing in the doorway, shoulders back, and for the first time realized how like Mary she was. Not in appearance but in stalwartness of character, courageous acceptance of reality without bemoaning.

The bottom had dropped out of Susan's world. Whether or not she knew the circumstances leading up to Rosamond's death, she must be all but over-powered by grief. Nor would it be unnatural if she gave a thought to the shattering of her own daydreams. Yet she spoke only of ranch affairs, said matter-of-factly Johnny's mother and stepfather had gone shopping in Moose for western clothes. She was going to take them for a ride this afternoon.

"You've got a splendid inheritance, Susan," I broke in, uttering aloud what was in my mind, the way one does after a sleeping pill.

She flushed. The deep rose of her sun-tanned cheek became crimson. "I don't take any stock in all that family stuff," she said. "Who cares how grand the Sloans used to be!"

"That wasn't what I meant at all."

She gave me no chance to explain. "I'm glad I was born in Wyoming. I'd hate to be anything but a Westerner," she added for good measure.

Then as if challenging me to disapprove, she said, "And I'm going to go to the state university at Laramie this fall, too. That's where Mother wanted to go. She—she's kept her application blank all these years. It won't cost much there. Besides, I can get some sort of job to help out, waiting on tables, at least."

"I think it's a wonderful idea," I said. "I congratulate you."

Mentally I congratulated her even more warmly when Jim came in after she'd departed and relayed his news.

A vast amount had been happening during these hours I'd wasted in sleep. Jim made no mention of Rosamond, yet I realized as he told me of those happenings, that her death, like a disaster of Nature's, fire or flood or earthquake, had served as a catalytic agent. Precipitated a profound upheaval in the lives of everyone close to her.

"We've been having a powwow over in Mary's and Brad's cabin," Jim began. "With Mary sitting up in bed like a queen bee." He laughed. "If a queen bee ever sits up in bed wearing an old corduroy hunting jacket."

The powwow had started as a business conference, which David had asked Jim to attend in a legal capacity. Whatever David's inner desolation, his outward manner had been admirably brisk.

David's Gethsemane, I thought, had been reached Saturday night. The anguish he'd suffered then at discovering his daughter's plans had immunized him against lesser grief.

In any event, David had told Brad and Mary this morning that he was prepared to finance the ranch project. They could go into Jackson today and get the deal sewn up.

Mary and Brad simultaneously, without needing to consult each other privately, had refused even to consider David's offer. Grateful they were, but adamant.

Convinced of their earnestness, David had then made a counter proposition. What about their moving to Ohio and Brad's taking a job at his plant?

As Jim could testify, David had long been searching for an administrative assistant of a particular kind. In Brad he'd found who would exactly fill the bill.

"He will, too," Jim assured me. "Visiting firemen come from all parts of the globe to see the plant. Brad will be the ideal man to take over their guidance and entertainment. Mary broke down and cried."

"At the thought of leaving here?"

"No. At the thought of Brad's getting an honest to God job, no charity involved. For the first time in his life Brad can be really self-respecting, earn a decent living."

"Oh, you mean she cried with joy."

"Yes, my poor dim-witted darling."

"How does she feel about Susan's staying on in Wyoming and going to the state university?"

"You know Mary well enough to know that if she feels any pangs, she's not going to admit it. She's proud of Susan's wanting to get an education by her own efforts. That much is plain.

"I'll tell you who really was rocked back on his heels, though. Our young Harvard friend. Amos had been all agog at the idea of Susan's living right there in Ohio where he'll be. When she calmly announced that she was staying out in God's country, instead, it was like a bombshell. You wouldn't have called him phlegmatic if you'd seen him then. Right in front of all of us, he asked Susan to marry him."

Jim had difficulty in not laughing out loud as he described Susan's reaction.

She had been extremely dignified. One corner of her shirttail was hanging out, yet even as she tucked it in she had been extremely dignified.

"Thank you very much," she said. "But I don't intend to marry anyone for ages and ages. Not until I'm twenty-one at least."

"Practically senile," I said.

Jim nodded. "That was the way she made it sound. Amos didn't give up easily, though. He begged her to change her mind. She really floored him then, the little devil. She said sweetly, 'Why, Amos, you yourself have shown me how much there is I don't know. I should think you of all people would understand why I want to go to college.'"

"Good for her!"

"Good for both of them, I'd say, in the unlikely event that anyone asked my opinion." Jim took the remaining piece of toast from the covered dish on my tray, spread it with marmalade and ate it with patent contentment.

"Lunch may be late," he said then. "David and Brad have gone into town to make long-distance calls and so on. David also needs some more drafting paper. He's been busy with plans for that new house he's finally going to build. A considerable distance from his mother-in-law's monstrosity. A place where Dorothy can rule the roost."

"It's too late," I said. "Dorothy's growing up fast. What with one thing and another, the silver cord's worn pretty thin."

"There I agree. In fact I suspect that before many moons have waxed and waned Dorothy's going to be more interested in furnishing a doctor's office. She'd probably indignantly deny it now, but the symptoms are clear to old Dr. Anthony. She and Kevin's sister hit it off right away."

Jim glanced out the open door, smiled with such lively approval I assumed he'd caught sight of Dorothy and Kevin. As indeed he had, I found. They were not alone, however; Johnny's mother and her husband were with them; all four were on their way to the swimming pool.

An ideal place to be with the noon sun blazing hot. I needed no urging to change into a bathing suit.

It was while I was searching for my bathing cap that I remembered Johnny.

The latest bulletin was not encouraging, Jim admitted; Johnny was still apathetic, unwilling to leave his cabin, unwilling to talk. Neither his mother nor anyone else had been able to get a word out of him.

Kevin had repeated the term emotional block; but confessed his inability to dislodge it. Spike's death had freed Johnny from the physical terror Spike had deliberately engendered, doubtless to rid himself of the boy's embarrassing presence while he was making preparations to decamp. And yesterday morning, when Mrs. Pritchett had discovered Spike's lifeless body in the darkened bedroom of the bunkhouse, she had kept Johnny from seeing it. Although even if she'd not acted so quickly, there could have been no visual shock to him; he would have seen nothing, save a man presumably asleep. Kevin himself had needed the aid of bright light to detect the small stain on the wine-colored shirt.

Johnny's trouble was only partially connected with Spike, I thought; it was rooted deep in his own miserable sense of insecurity, his consuming jealousy of his new stepsister. But I had no desire to state this theory, to describe the ferocity with which he had defaced the photograph of his new stepsister; his threats of personal violence if she ever dared come out here.

My heart skipped a beat as I heard a squeal from the porch next door. A small girl's squeal.

Johnny had threatened to scalp Constance. Yet they'd left him alone with her.

Our side window was open. Through it I had an unimpeded view.

The squeal, I perceived, had been one of pure delight.

"And then what happened?" Constance asked eagerly.

Like a miniature elderly couple, Johnny was seated in a large rawhide chair, Constance in a smaller one facing him, her round cherubic countenance upturned to his. Two short braids tied with red ribbon hung over the shoulders of her plaid shirt; she wore brand-new blue jeans, several sizes too large, midget-sized cowboy boots with red tops.

I listened shamelessly, Jim at my shoulder.

Johnny said, "I knew Mrs. Pritchett was scared. She's sort of the housekeeper, see? So I put down the telephone and went right up to Spike's door."

Well, so he had, I remembered. That had been extraordinarily brave of him, in view of Spike's threats.

"I saw the shine of a gun," Johnny continued, embroidering copiously, like many a brave man before him. "But that didn't stop me. I said, 'Wake up, you dastardly wall-eyed jughead!' And I shook him hard."

Johnny hesitated, then presumably inspired by the breathlessness of his auditor, soared to giddier heights.

"I looked at my hands. They were as red as your hair-ribbons, Constance. There was blood on the floor, and blood on the bed. I guess there wasn't an inch of me that wasn't covered with blood."

Constance, the pink-cheeked little angel, fairly crowed with joy.

The pause now was longer. Understandably Johnny's powers of invention were almost exhausted. He was normally an exceptionally truthful boy. He rallied, however.

"Spike was a bad man, Constance. A very very bad man. It's dangerous out here. A lot more dangerous than Paris, France."

She shivered, her eyes grew wider.

And at this, having made his point, established the superiority of his environment, responsibility descended upon Johnny.

Up to now the only child on the ranch, he'd been treated as if he were younger than his actual age of ten. But this small girl was four years younger. By comparison he was grown up.

I'd guessed wrong about other people, other things, but this time I knew I was right; knew that Johnny was creating for himself the only kind of security that endures, when I heard him say gravely, protectively, leaning forward to emphasize his seriousness, "That was just sort of a story I—I made up, see? There's nothing for you to be scared of out here, Constance. I know the ropes and I'll take care of you."

BRUTAL Question

by OLIVER WELD BAYER

author of "AN EYE FOR AN EYE"

Crime is of the Essence

Joe Csida

DEATH BEATS THE BAND

IDA SHURMAN

MURDER AT DRAKE'S ANCHORAGE

E. LEE WADDELL

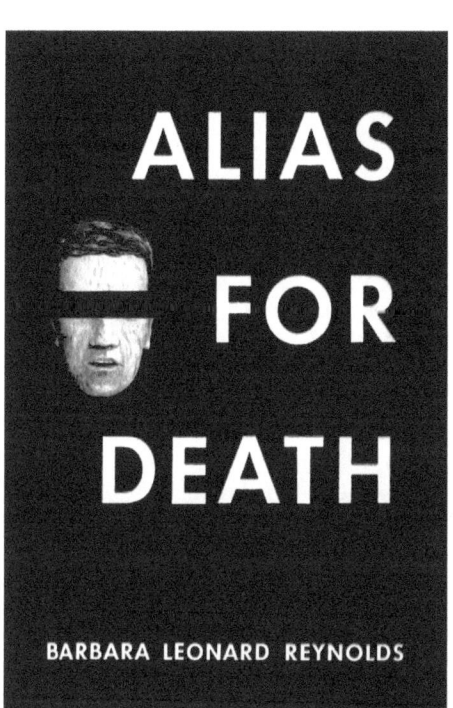

ALIAS
FOR
DEATH

BARBARA LEONARD REYNOLDS

MURDER
AT GLEN ATHOL

NORMAN LIPPINCOTT

A strange clan—a grotesque dinner party—and
violent death in a little Pennsylvania town!

MURDER
À LA RICHELIEU
THE ADELAIDE ADAMS MYSTERIES
ANITA BLACKMON

THERE IS
NO RETURN
THE ADELAIDE ADAMS MYSTERIES
ANITA BLACKMON

MARIAN GALLAGHER SCOTT

DEAD HANDS REACHING

DEATH'S LONG SHADOW

MARIAN GALLAGHER SCOTT

TALL MAN WALKING

THE ATTIC ROOM

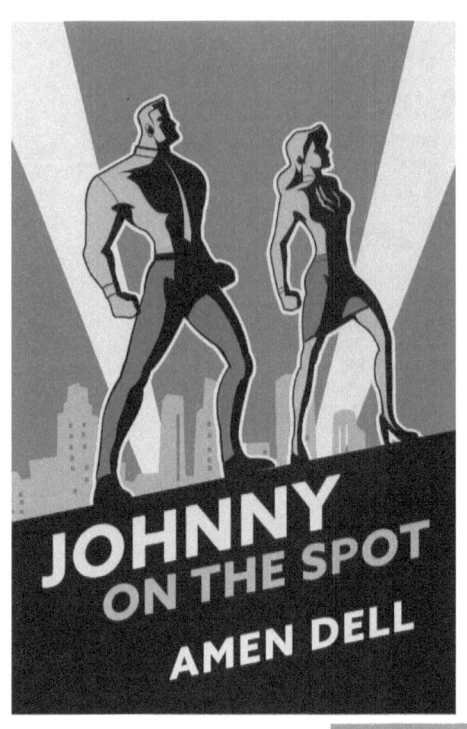

JOHNNY
ON THE SPOT
AMEN DELL

CRIME IN
CORN-WEATHER

MARY MEIGS ATWATER

THE
MUSEUM
MURDER

JOHN T. McINTYRE

KILL 'EM
WITH
KINDNESS

By
FRED DICKENSON

MURDER ENDS THE SONG

ALFRED MEYERS

MURDER A LA MODE

ELEANORE KELLY SELLARS

CLASSIC RED BADGE PRIZE MYSTERY

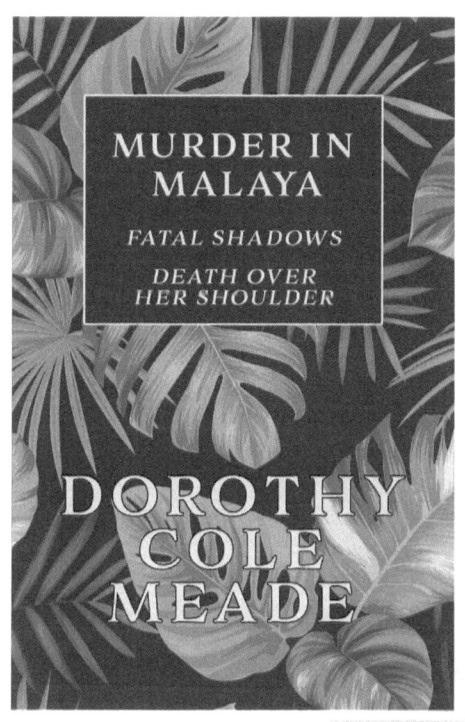

MURDER IN MALAYA

FATAL SHADOWS

DEATH OVER HER SHOULDER

DOROTHY COLE MEADE

MURDER IN A WALLED TOWN

KATHERINE WOODS

DETECTIVES 4

MISS MADELYN MACK
HUGH C. WEIR

MISS VAN SNOOP
CLARENCE ROOK

VIOLET STRANGE
ANNA KATHARINE GREEN

FLORENCE CUSACK
MEADE & EUSTACE

DETECTIVES 2

LOVEDAY BROOKE
CATHERINE LOUISA PIRKIN

LADY MOLLY OF SCOTLAND YARD
BARONESS EMMA ORCZY

DETECTIVES 4

BROMLEY BARNES
GEORGE BARTON

TRENT'S LAST CASE
E. C. BENTLEY

KALA PERSAD
HEADON HILL

GALLAGHER
RICHARD HARDING DAVIS

DETECTIVES 3

AN ARISTOCRATIC DETECTIVE
RICHARD MARSH

JANE SPROOD, DETECTIVE
ELLIS PARKER BUTLER

THE DELIBERATE DETECTIVE
E. PHILLIPS OPPENHEIM